The Enchanted World

THE SECRET ARTS

The Enchanted World :

THE SECRET ARTS /

by the Editors of Time-Life Books

The Content

Time-Life Books · Alexandria, Virginia

Chapter One

The Power of the Word

Insatiable in their lust for knowledge, the practitioners of magic yearned to see beyond the tangible world, to learn the secret laws that governed the fates of souls and nations. In every age, scholars sought to piece together fragments of these hidden truths, and to grant themselves a kind of immortality by preserving their hard-won discoveries for adepts as yet unborn.

Their messages took different forms. Fragile baked-clay tablets bore cuneiform impressions made with reed pens when the clay was new and soft. Carved hieroglyphic charms were sealed in the changeless air of Pharaohs' underground tombs. Shreds of papyrus lay deep under hot sands that over the centuries crept whispering away, revealing the scrolls finally to the eyes of mystified herdsmen. Tall sentinel stones inscribed with spidery runes wept with the gentle rain that soaked the hillsides where they stood. Heavy volumes with black-lettered pages were chained out of sight in monastic libraries. Encap-

The secret script of Egypt's priestly mages

For the scribes of ancient Egypt, the written word, whether set down on papyrus or etched in stone, was a gift from the gods. But hieroglyphs were more than abstract symbols. Each one embodied the very spirit of the object it represented. Eternal life could be gained, or an enemy's spirit destroyed, by the judicious use of these figures.

The most powerful of all the hieroglyphs was the ankh, a looped cross that symbolized life itself. A Pharaoh anxious to protect himself after death from the ravages of grave robbers or the envy of ambitious relatives could ensure his soul's survival by instructing the painter of his tomb to depict him with the sacred ankh held beneath his nose, seat of the body's vital forces. So long as the image remained undisturbed, his spirit would live on, inhaling the very breath of life.

sulated in silent characters, the words waited, charged with arcane powers.

To those adventurers who would crack their codes, the chroniclers passed on a caveat: The secrets of the universe were not lightly disclosed; any unworthy soul who probed too deep risked an unspeakable fate. Yet the lure of knowledge often overcame the dictates of caution.

One seeker who could not quit the quest despite the cost was Prince Nefrekeptah, son of an eighteenth-dynasty Pharaoh and an accomplished sorcerer in his own right. Dedicated to the pursuit of occult wisdom, he spent his days studying the texts that were carved on the walls of the temples and within the pyramids of Egypt's long-dead Kings.

It happened once in an ancient shrine at Memphis, when the Prince was pursuing his researches, that a harsh laugh interrupted his concentration. He turned from the hieroglyphs he was transcribing to find that a temple priest stood watching him. The man asked Nefrekeptah why he wasted his time on trivialities when, if he wished, he could go straight to the fountainhead of all knowledge.

Nefrekeptah's pulse raced. He knew that the priest meant the Book of Thoth, written by the deity of that name, patron of wisdom and scribe of the gods, the inventor of speech itself. The Book's forty-two scrolls contained all the wisdom of the world. The very first lines imparted to the reader an understanding of the languages of all living creatures; the next passage revealed the secrets of the divinities, and all that was hidden in the stars. The pages that followed contained revel-

ations far beyond the comprehension of all but the most gifted initiates. Every scholar spoke of this legendary text, but none had ever seen it.

Nefrekeptah immediately offered any price for knowledge of the Book's whereabouts. All the priest asked in payment was a hundred bars of silver and a burial with royal privileges. This granted, he told the Pharaoh's son that the Book lay in the innermost casket of a nested series of boxes sunk in the Nile at Koptos, far to the south. Reptiles and scorpions surrounded it, and a deathless serpent protected it from thieves.

Nefrekeptah brought this news to his wife, Ahura, who, according to pharaonic custom, was also his sister. She was the companion of his heart in everything, and the mother of Merab, his idolized young son. Convinced that evil would come of her husband's fanatical pursuit of knowledge, Ahura begged him to desist. But Nefrekeptah ignored her. From the Pharaoh, father to them both, he begged for the use of the royal barge. With Ahura and Merab, he sailed to Koptos in search of the Book.

At Koptos he settled his wife and son in a riverside palace, and went alone to the bank of the Nile to begin his preparations. If the fishermen had looked up from their nets, or the peasants from their fields, they would have seen something wonderful and strange. For Nefrekeptah conjured out of nothing a small house, no larger than the inner chamber of a tomb. With whispered

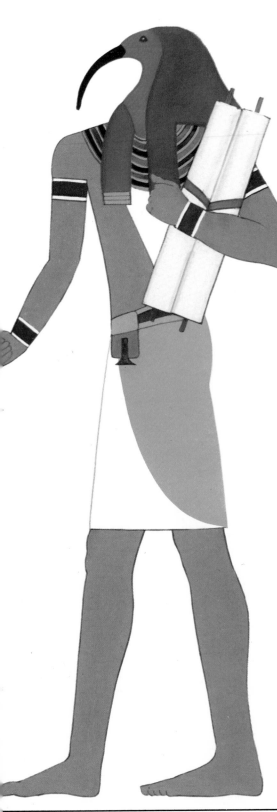

spells he created an army of small statues, men in miniature, and imbued them with life. Then he set them all to work.

Some were commanded to load the barge up with sand from the riverbank, which they did with an alacrity that no human laborer, many times their size, could equal. The others Nefrekeptah ordered into the little house, which, by means of spells and with the aid of a stout rope, he proceeded to lower— inch by inch—until it rested on the bottom of the Nile. With solemn words of invocation, the sorcerer-prince called on his creatures to search the riverbed until they found the Book of Thoth, and at once they appeared, shimmering under the surface, as at home in water as in air. After three days and nights of painstaking toil, one of them swam up through the water to tell Nefrekeptah that the Book had been found.

Smiling at his own cunning, Nefrekeptah called out again and the small creatures began to shovel the sand from the barge into the river, spadeful by spadeful, forming a shoal that gradually rose up toward the light and broke the surface of the water. Step by step, the miniature slaves pushed their prize up the underwater hill of sand until finally, alive with writhing reptiles and scorpions, the box containing the Book of Thoth emerged into daylight. The serpent that could not die lay coiled around it.

Nefrekeptah stepped from the riverbank onto the shoal. With a cry of command, he struck the snakes and scorpions into immobility. However, the great serpent was immune to spells as well as

The ancient Egyptians revered the Ibis-headed deity Thoth, inventor of the art of writing, who had recorded on scrolls all the secrets of the universe.

Learning that the Book of Thoth lay buried beneath the Nile, one intrepid seeker after truth used his magical prowess to create an army of manikins who could labor in the watery depths. They searched until they unearthed a chest containing the precious text.

to physical assaults; when Nefrekeptah smote off its head, the two parts instantly drew toward each other. But the Prince was as quick-witted as he was skilled in the magic arts, and by sealing the cut surfaces of the snake's body and head with sand, he prevented the two pieces from knitting together. Helpless at last, the box's faithful guardian lay inanimate, its muscular coils slack and useless, as its conqueror rifled the treasure that it had watched since the dawn of time.

Just as the priest had described, each box concealed another. The outermost was of iron, the next bronze, the third wrought of sycamore wood. Inside it was a case of exquisite workmanship, made of ivory and ebony, containing a silver casket that itself enclosed a box fashioned from gold.

Opening them with trembling fingers, Nefrekeptah at last set eyes upon his treasure: the forty-two small scrolls that made up the Book of Thoth. He took the first scroll in his hands and scanned it. Then he raised his head. All at once he understood the calls of the water birds and the language of the land creatures. Even the hissing of snakes had meaning. He read on, then gazed up at the heavens, and knew the secrets of the stars.

Clutching his prize, Nefrekeptah hurried back to Ahura. Thrusting the scrolls at her, he implored her to cast her eyes over the first lines. The woman recoiled at the sight, as if the snakes and scorpions still writhed around the scrolls. But she yielded to her husband's entreaties. And within moments, she too possessed the miraculous knowledge.

But it did her little good, for Nefrekeptah committed an act of sacrilege that called down wrath upon their heads. To make the spells his own, he copied them on sheets of papyrus. Over the writing he poured barley beer, so that the ink, still wet, mingled with the brew, and ran down the pages into a cup. Raising the vessel to his lips, the Prince imbibed the liquid, and thus took the magic words into his own body. Triumphant, he offered a draught to Ahura, but she clamped her lips together and shook her head in anguished refusal.

Punishment came swiftly. The family set off for Memphis; but the royal barge they sat in swung around in the water, to float above the spot where the Book had rested. As it hovered, the little boy Merab rose from his place, as if in a dream, and walked straight off the deck into the water, where he sank from sight. With trembling hands Nefrekeptah found a spell in the Book of Thoth that drew the child's body to the surface. But no magic existed that could bring him back to life.

Shattered, Nefrekeptah and Ahura returned to shore to bury their child according to the ancient rites. At last they set out again to bring their father the news of their misfortune. But when they came to the place where Merab had died, Ahura too was drawn, entranced and unresisting, out of the boat to drown in the river. A second time, Nefrekeptah used his sorcery to redeem the body from the water, but he could not restore his beloved to life. He returned to Koptos once

Having vanquished the serpents and scorpions that guarded the Book,
    the scholar devoured the scrolls with his eyes. Instantly, he found he
could see the immortal gods and understand the language of the beasts.

more, borne down by grief, to bury his wife beside their child.

A third time, Nefrekeptah set out for Memphis. As his barge progressed along the waterway, many people paused in their labors—farmers and fishermen, carpenters and scribes, cooks and priests—to watch the scion of Egypt's royal house pass by. But Nefrekeptah never appeared on deck, no banners fluttered, and no rowers chanted as the barge slid silently between the reed-fringed banks. Some folk claimed, much later, that they had heard inhuman noises emanating from the craft: hissing, wailing, screams and howls. After a long, slow voyage, the boat arrived at last at Egypt's capital city and the Pharaoh came on board to greet his son. But all was silent. In the cabin lay the corpse of Nefrekeptah, its sightless eyes open wide. On his breast were draped the scrolls of the Book of Thoth.

So was Nefrekeptah destroyed for his presumption in appropriating the book of all books, which contained in its purest form the body of knowledge that gave power over the whole of creation. But his fate deterred few. In every age appeared power-seekers ready to risk everything to gain possession of the priceless discoveries of vanished masters, ready to follow up the slightest rumor that might lead them to the secrets of ages past.

Diverse figures stood in Nefrekeptah's succession: stiff-bearded Assyrian sorcerers, turning their eyes to the heavens; wizened sibyls in sacred groves, reeling from narcotic fumes as they strove to hold the truths that they had glimpsed through the rents in their consciousness; Celtic seers crooning for long nights in the smoky gloom of rainswept hovels; gowned scholars solitary at midnight behind the tall, leaded windows of medieval castles, appalled but unflinching in their obsessional quest; Moorish philosophers working quietly in the austere peace of marbled Cordoban courts.

One of the greatest of the inquirers into such mysteries was the Renaissance polymath Heinrich Cornelius Agrippa von Nettesheim, whose life was spent searching tirelessly through the works of ancient and modern writers to perfect his own system of occult philosophy. If any man deserved to partake of mystic knowledge it was he, for his scholarship was boundless and his respect for the unseen powers profound.

But in his house, the story was told, there lodged a student who possessed none of the master's wisdom. One day, when the great man was away from home, the student managed to slip into Agrippa's study. The young meddler read the open pages of the book on the lectern, then turned the leaves (made, it was whispered afterward, of dead men's skin) in awestruck fascination. So absorbed was he that at first he was not aware of another figure in the room. When he did look up, he nearly died of fright, for there stood before him a demon—it might have been the Devil himself—who demanded to know why he had been sent for. The student had no answer but a gasp of horror, and the demon throttled him on the spot, leaving his corpse as a warning

Inscriptions charged with occult force

Odin, father and chief of the Norse gods, passed on his knowledge of magic and rune-lore to poets, sorcerers, sages and other especially favored mortals. The runes in his gift constituted an alphabet for writing. But they were far more than mere symbols: Initiates knew them as actual sources of power—tools and weapons of wizardry.

Those who understood the secrets of the runes knew the proper figures to inscribe on a sword to protect its owner in battle, or which runes to carve on a tombstone to keep evil spirits at bay. The cunning of some runemasters ran so deep that their inscriptions could even control the dead, preventing a restless corpse from rising and wandering, or causing a hanged man to walk and speak.

But men of such prodigious power inspired more fear than admiration in Europe's dark ages of rival cults and warring tribes. Kings and priests looked upon them with suspicion. In some lands the very possession of a tablet filled with wonder-working runes became a punishable crime. Adepts were burned to death, and their knowledge disappeared with them. In the remotest regions, their carved stones survived as objects of mystery and menace. But the real power of the runes was lost forever.

against interference with the dangerous powers contained in books. Agrippa, it was said, took no more students into his house from that day forward.

The country people of Brittany, in former times, knew all too well the perils that attended books, and would have been glad to have had nothing to do with the insidious objects. But, against their will, these folk were the guardians of certain volumes of great antiquity and power which were known, after the famous philosopher, as Agrippas. Originally the Agrippas had resided in the keeping of the priests to whom the peasants looked for spiritual protection. While the books lay safely under lock and key in monastic libraries, the holy aura of the Church sufficed to contain the demonic forces bottled within them. But in a troubled era, when the Church was torn by strife and its priests scattered, some of the Agrippas found their way into the possession of ordinary families, who were left to cope unaided with the dark, intricate knowledge from a vanished age.

The potency of an Agrippa came from the fact that it was signed by the Devil himself. Its text listed the names of all demons, and indicated the services they could perform for humankind: the gratification of lusts, the acquisition of knowledge otherwise forbidden and of wealth untold. More perilously, it gave instructions for summoning these infernal servants. Hence it was possible to tell if a person had opened an Agrippa, even if he tried to keep it a secret: The sulfurous breath of devils and the smoke of Hel lingered on his hair and clothes.

An Agrippa, it seemed, was itself a demon. The book was of enormous size, as tall as a man. It was a living thing, with a will and a stubborn temper of its own. It violently resented being consulted, and would only submit after a long and exhausting struggle. And even if the owner forbore to open the book's covers, its unpredictable rages meant that it was a perpetual danger. It could destroy the building that housed it or drive its owner mad, for it had all the heat and fury of hellfire bound up within its pages. Sages suggested that the only way to ensure it did no harm was to keep it padlocked, hanging by a chain from a twisted beam in an otherwise empty room. But few who owned an Agrippa could resist the curiosity that compelled them toward it.

The possession of an Agrippa, with all the troubles that it brought, was a life sentence—or worse than that. When its owner was dying, the Agrippa, sensing abandonment, would create a terrible uproar, driving the farm animals to a frenzy, shaking the stone walls of the house and its outbuildings. The only force that could stop it was a ritual exorcism by the parish priest. Instructed by the cleric, the family would light a pile of straw and haul the Agrippa onto the flames. The great book would burn with a fierce heat, and soon be consumed to ashes. These the priest would meticulously gather up into a little pouch, which he would hang around the dying man's neck and bury with him to rid the survivors of any residual affliction, and to free them for all time from the curse of such a dangerous possession.

In Penvenan, close to the Brittany coast, where the gales swept in off the Atlantic, there lived a stout-hearted man who once tried to rid himself of the stubborn Agrippa that had been in his family for generations. But he succeeded only in proving the book's implacable power.

Loizo-goz was a Breton of taciturn determination and much physical strength. The huge, rebellious Agrippa in his house had become such a nuisance to him that he could tolerate its presence no longer. He called on a nearby farmer who, according to local gossip, dabbled in magic. Loizo-goz raised the topic circumspectly. Finding the man intrigued, even envious, of his possession and not at

ABRACADABRA
ABRACADABR
ABRACADAB
ABRACADA
ABRACAD
ABRACA
ABRAC
ABRA
ABR
AB
A

A hoary charm from magic's morning

Healers traveling with the Roman legions used the ancient Hebrew name of power, Abracadabra, to make a fever-conquering spell. The letters were arranged in an inverted triangle, beginning with the whole word and ending with a single letter. The word was begun anew on every line, each time losing the last of its letters until only one, "A", remained. The fever was supposed to imitate the decreasing number of letters by gradually waning away.

To effect the cure, the physician set the spell, written on parchment, around the invalid's neck for nine days. At the end of that time, it was removed and flung over the victim's shoulder into an eastward-flowing stream. The rushing waters drew the heat of the infection away from the patient and back to the rising sun, source of all warmth, thus completing the treatment.

The priests of Brittany in bygone days took charge of certain books of fiendish character, wherein were recorded the manners of summoning devils. The books were prone to run amok unless suspended by a chain and secured with a stout padlock.

all worried by its well-known perils, he offered the farmer the book. To his relief, the gift was accepted.

A few nights later, everyone in the district heard a terrible din. It was Loizo-goz, dragging his complaining Agrippa by its chain to his neighbor's farm. He managed to manhandle the resisting bulk to the farmer's house, and together the two men forced it into an attic room.

When the door was locked upon it they went downstairs to the spacious, low-ceilinged kitchen, where the farmer poured two much-needed tots of brandy to revive them. Few words were exchanged, and Loizo-goz did not stay long. When at last the farmhouse door swung to behind him and he heard its heavy bolt fall into place, he pursed his usually grim lips and whistled a snatch of an old Breton folktune.

As he entered his own house, however, his mood darkened. He went to the door of the room where the Agrippa had been imprisoned. He opened it a crack, but he already knew what he would see. There was the great black book, hanging once more from its crooked beam and turning slowly on its stout chain.

Loizo-goz grew desperate. He made a huge fire and heaved the book onto the pyre. But the flames, although they burned as brightly as ever, drew away from the book and would not touch it. When the fire had burned itself out, the Agrippa's cover hardly felt warm.

Since fire had proved no help, Loizo-goz resolved to try water. He hauled the book down to the beach, where he tied to it several stones as large as he could lift. Somehow he got the whole cumbersome bundle into his boat and put out to sea with it. Once in deep water he hoisted the weighted book out of the boat. It sank and the water closed over it.

As he beached the boat, he glanced back over his shoulder, and what he saw froze his blood. The book had risen again. At incredible speed, it glided toward the shore. Its chain rasped on the pebbles as it passed him on the beach and sped toward the house. Just as he had expected, when Loizo-goz reached home, the Agrippa was hanging once more by its chain. Its cover was bone dry, its pages did not even smell of the sea. Unbeliever though he was, he finally turned to the Church to help him. But each time he tried to summon the priest, some accident ensured that his message was not received. First he sent a farmhand to deliver his plea, but halfway to the church the man fell off his horse and broke his neck. Next, Loizo-goz went himself to beg for aid, but found the cleric had died the night before. He tried again with the new incumbent, and found himself paralyzed with a sudden seizure before he could give voice to his request. He died soon after, but the Agrippa's brooding presence so darkened his house that no one would live in it from that day forward.

While the possession of an Agrippa meant unmitigated misery for a layman and heavy cares even for a priest, many magical writings were treasured allies in the struggle of good against evil. Their words recorded the formulas to control

A Breton farmer unfortunate enough to possess one of the devilish books strove to rid himself of his burden. But when he tried to drown it, it rose from the waves and pursued him shoreward.

unruly forces, and the letters themselves pulsed with virtuous energy.

Icelandic bards told of a benevolent wizard named Eirikur who owned such a magical tome, and used it to help his countrymen when dark powers threatened them. One of his clients was a young farmer from the Vestmanna Islands off the mainland's southern coast. Seven weeks after their wedding, the farmer's bride had risen early one morning and gone out, as usual, to fetch the firewood. She never returned. The farmer searched everywhere, but could discover no sign of her. Picturing her drowned beneath the cold sea that beat upon the island from every side, he fell into such a black slough that his friends began to fear for his life. They advised him to sustain hope a little longer, and urged him to consult Eirikur.

When the farmer arrived at the seer's house on the mainland, he found he was expected: The wise man's first words were an inquiry about the missing bride. The seer promised to put his skills at the wretched husband's disposal.

For three days Eirikur studied his book, but made no move. Then on a morning of foul weather he led the farmer on horseback to a pile of great rocks on a lonely hillside. He leaned the book against the largest of the ancient stones, and although the storm billowed about them, the volume remained dry and unspotted, and its leaves never stirred.

Eirikur stared intently at the book as if sucking sustenance from its pages. Then he walked around the rock, moving, in the time-honored manner of the sorcerer, anticlockwise, and uttered a spell.

As the magician murmured, figures emerged from the living rock and crowded together on the grass. These, said Eirikur, were mortals who had been spirited to the otherworld by trolls. He bade the farmer look carefully to see whether his wife was one of them. The farmer walked through the silent figures, scanning their impassive faces. His bride was not there. The wizard gravely thanked the revenants for answering his call, and they vanished into the rock.

Again, Eirikur turned to his book, found a new place in it, then paced his way around the rock, murmuring. A different group of people drifted from the rock, but the farmer's wife was not among them. Eirikur tried once more, and once more failed. The seer, pale and weary, confessed that he had called every troll in Iceland, and now knew nowhere to turn. Suddenly his eyes lit up.

Eirikur recalled one pair of trolls who had not been named in his spells. He drew from his robe a single page of antique writing. Unfolding the parchment, he laid it upon the open book and softly read out a spell. Out of the rock came a pair of hideous creatures carrying a glass cage. Within it was the figure of a woman only inches high. The farmer cried out. The tiny creature was his wife.

With words of power, Eirikur rebuked the trolls and drove them back to their own dark world. As they vanished, the glazed box shattered on the ground, and Eirikur lifted away the shards to release

With a whispered spell, a wise man of Iceland summoned a troll couple
who had stolen a farmer's bride. They emerged from the earth carrying
the young woman, still alive, but shrunken and imprisoned in glass.

A calligraphic cure for stomach pains

In the age when few could read, writing was deemed to possess uncanny powers. A written spell to overcome illness might work with more force than spoken magic, especially if the words remained in physical contact with the sufferer.

The people of early England cherished a formula against stomach ailments that bore vestiges of the languages of the ancients—Hebrew, Aramaic, Latin and Greek. Tradition held that the charm had been brought down from heaven by an angel. The spell began with an incantation meaning "Shout, the Lord is my shield," and ended with the cry "Alleluiah, Alleluiah." In between came a babble of incoherent words, that made neither sentences nor sense.

When written on a long, narrow strip of parchment and bound around the sufferer's head, the age-old words were charged with power. The magically inscribed paper was said to cure the patient promptly.

the prisoner. At first she remained unnaturally small, as if seen from a great height; Eirikur read a passage from his book and she grew to her proper size, then collapsed into her husband's arms.

For safety's sake the wise man journeyed with the couple back to their own island. Trolls robbed of their prizes could be vengeful. He stayed for three days, lying each night with his head pillowed on his book at the door of their house, listening to the sounds outside. What he heard was neither the pounding of the waves nor the calling of seabirds, but the sibilant whispers of an inhuman hate. The trolls, unwilling to accept defeat, had come back to claim their slave.

They lurked outside the door of the house, peered through the windows with eyes red and malevolent, muttered threats and curses through the chinks in the wall. But Eirikur drew strength from the book that was his pillow. He rose up and from his parted lips there issued a spell so terrible that it turned the night sky white, and sent the trollish kidnappers squealing back to the netherworld. Hearing this tale, the women on Iceland's farms walked warily, knowing that somewhere, on a lonely shore or at the foot of a black volcano, a pair of disgruntled trolls were on the hunt for a new slave.

Eirikur's book imparted much of its magic directly, through physical contact, just as the spells in the Book of Thoth had entered Nefrekeptah in the beer he gulped. Many other writings possessed such concrete powers. Magical inscriptions carved on stone in ancient Egypt sometimes incorporated channels to collect water that was poured over the text to absorb its virtue; it could be brewed into efficacious potions. Chinese talismans of ivory and jade, inscribed with the ideograms for happiness, long life, peace or prosperity, were worn to confer their meanings upon their possessors. In a similar vein, when a patient consulted a healer in Anglo-Saxon England, he might receive a spell written down on a scrap of parchment, to be bound like a poultice over the afflicted part.

Yet for many purposes, the spoken word possessed greater powers than the written. A name, once pronounced, evoked its owner; anyone who was foolhardy enough to utter the name of a person deceased could expect to be visited by his or her spirit.

Gods, too, could be summoned by the utterance of a name, and since a god was likely to be angered if invoked for a trivial cause, many peoples kept the names of the beings they worshiped a hallowed secret. Curses and blessings likewise harnessed the power of the spoken word. As a curse was uttered, it released supernatural powers against those named; a blessing channeled a deity's beneficence.

But most spells had to be spoken aloud to be effective. English rustics addressed a verse to swarming bees to discourage them from leaving home, and throughout medieval Europe, repetition of the Lord's Prayer was a trusted cure for warts.

Some spells had to be chanted; others, such as Eirikur's invocation of the trolls' victims, were to be murmured in a low

voice so that the formulas could not be overheard. In most spells, furthermore, the words had to be spoken in precisely the right rhythm and tone. It profited a scholar little to know the secret words of power if, when he uttered them, he could not make the correct sounds to conjure their meanings out of the air.

If a wizard who wanted to fly as fast as the speediest hawk followed to the letter the instructions given in his handbook of magic—if he boiled snow and oil together on a fire of two kinds of wood, ripened it in a sheep's bladder for a moon and a half, mingled it with charcoal, then powdered the charcoal and placed a pinch of the powder between the pages of a book, took the book in his hand and concentrated his whole attention on his destination—what good was all that if he did not know how to pronounce the essential words SISPI SISPI that the spell prescribed? If that seemed simple enough, and he did indeed find himself far away, could he be sure that when he read off the returning charm, ITTSS ITTSS, he would hit on the right sound and not sentence himself to permanent exile?

Words, indeed, were powerful, even perilous. The common currency of human relations they might be, but they were also keys that fit an infinity of hidden locks, opening the doors of occult wisdom. The more an initiate knew of their potential, the more circumspect he or she became. Storytellers, recounting wonders, might wax loquacious. But a wizard, working wonders, kept silent, lest his secrets fall into unworthy hands, and all hell break loose in consequence.

A sure way to prevent swarming bees from leaving their hive was to throw sand at them and declaim a spell that began, "Settle, victorious women, sink down to earth. You must never fly wild to the wood."

Chapter Two

Decoding Destiny

The army would march with the dawn. All had been decided: The supply carts had been loaded and tallied by the quartermasters; the legate of each legion had addressed his cohort commanders and each centurion had his orders. The decurions had seen to the last issue of sour ration wine and checked the harnesses and the weapons of each of their men; in the cavalry lines, shivering troopers stood to beside their horses and gave their nervous, whinnying beasts such comfort as they could.

But it was not only the sunrise they awaited. No Roman army would set forth without more guidance than mere light of day could give it: First, it must know the will of the gods. A sign must be found and its meaning read by one steeped in mysterious lore. And now, before the assembled troops, the ritual ran its course.

Torches flared and smoked, lending a sullen gleam to the gilded eagles of the legions and the helms and breastplates of their expectant generals. His features concealed by the robes that marked his office, the haruspex began his

work. From the darkness beyond the torchlit circle, his servants brought him a sheep. The animal bleated in fear, but the haruspex stroked it with skilled fingers, and at last the creature stood quietly. It was as well: A sacrifice that came unwilling could grant no revelation.

The haruspex reached inside his robes. The waiting soldiers caught the flash of the knife as it swept across the animal's throat. The sheep crumpled with a sigh, and the haruspex kneeled beside it. Again the knife slashed. The animal's entire body heaved and bubbled.

Now the torchbearers crowded close around the diviner, centering him in a pool of yellow light. Without a word, he plunged his arms elbow-deep in the slit belly. For a moment, his fingers probed. Then he pulled once, sharply. The convoluted mass of the sheep's entrails slithered out onto the ground, rank and steaming in the night air.

The haruspex beckoned to a servant, and a torch was lowered. Expertly, he examined the folds and the loops and the random bunching of intestinal veins. His fingers sought out the warm, flopping liver, teasing meaning from the pattern of its lobes. Then he stood, wiped his hands upon his bloodstained robe and nodded to the commanding General. In turn, the General made a sign to the clerk of his treasury. The haruspex would be rewarded. All was as it should be. In the east, yellow began to streak the sky. Trumpets blared. Unit by unit, the great armed array wheeled off to meet its destiny.

To a skilled practitioner, the undulations of a plume of smoke conveyed hidden truths of things to come.

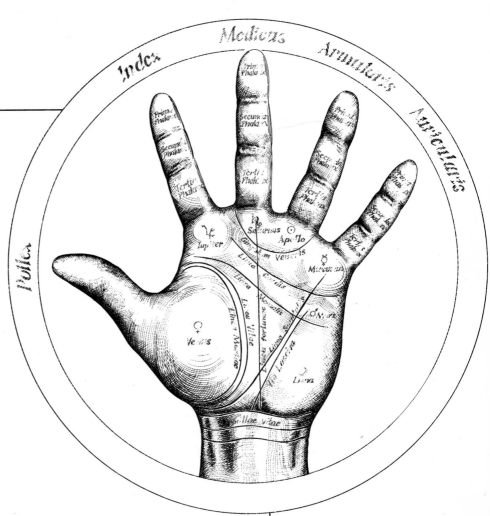

Haruspicy and hepatoscopy—the arts of predicting the future from the entrails and the liver of a slaughtered animal—were ancient before Rome was born. The Romans learned their skills from the Etruscans, whose vanished civilization once held sway between the River Tiber and the Alps that shielded their glittering cities from barbarian Europe. Perhaps the Etruscans' knowledge was a gift from their own dark, forgotten gods; perhaps it had come to them from Mesopotamia, where the first civilizations arose. In many-towered Babylon, mighty wizards used livers shaped from clay to teach the secrets of divination to their acolytes.

The word divination bespeaks the ultimate origins of the soothsayer's knowledge: the gods themselves, divinities who ruled all things. And for those who possessed talent, skill and learning, the knowledge could be found in all things, too. There was a unity in nature, the ancients reckoned, and nothing happened by chance. There were no causes and no effects; instead, everything—past, present and future—was bound into a seamless whole. By studying a tiny part of it, the great complexity might be revealed.

Haruspicy was only one of myriad routes to revelation. Signs and portents could be found everywhere by those who cared to look: from the shifting coils of smoke above a fire, or from the patterns formed by molten wax in water; by the progress of stars through the firmament, or by the flight of birds. The gods were generous with their clues.

To read the meanings, though, was seldom easy. The methods for doing so were numerous and, to the uninitiate, often bizarre. Their very names formed a litany of hidden learning. Practitioners of hydromancy cast pebbles into a pool and learned the future from the circles they made in the water. Alectoromancy required its adepts to study the movements of a white cockerel as it pecked grain from a magic circle inscribed on the earth. Those who were well versed in the skills of amniomancy could read the future in the birth-caul of a newborn child; and seers trained in the art of geloscopy learned much from the pitch and rhythm of a person's laughter.

The practitioners of chiromancy—the reading of hands—opened the book of fate by interpreting the lines, whorls and mounds of the human palm. To a chiromancer, these features represented an

Revelations writ in flesh

Would a life be long and healthy? Would a lover be constant till death? Would fortune favor a new enterprise? The cunning chiromancer could find the answers to all such questions, and many more, after brooding over an open hand and tracing the linea vitae, linea cordis, linea fortunae—the lines of life, the heart and fate—and other markings that formed the pattern of a palm. Both hands had to be studied, for the left told of original destiny, while the right revealed an individual's reactions to his fate.

The reading of hands was an art as old as civilization itself. The ancient Egyptians concealed a treatise on the subject in one of their pyramids. And it was said that sages recognized Buddha as their long-promised prophet at the moment of birth from a contemplation of the markings on his infant hands as well as those on the soles of his tiny feet.

account of their owner's past, present and future, written with the skin's own alphabet in a language whose intricate grammar had been studied for millennia throughout the world. Astragalomancy entailed the casting of lots—the knucklebones of sheep, sticks, pebbles or, in later ages, dice. Shaken and scattered, these tokens displayed seemingly random patterns that, if properly interpreted, could indicate the will of the gods.

But the gods could also make their wishes known by using human beings as their message-bearers. Throughout the ancient world, pilgrims sought out the sacred precincts that sheltered divinely appointed oracles. The most famous was at Delphi in Greece, reputedly the center of the world. Long ago, a temple was built there over a volcanic crack in the rock. Beside the fuming chasm, the appointed priestess—the "Pythoness," she was called, after a legendary snake that had once guarded the shrine—sat upon a tripod and did her visionary work. The sacredness of the place, as well as the laurel leaves she chewed and the subterranean vapors she inhaled, ensured that she was in a highly receptive trance. Initially, the Pythoness responded directly to her questioners; but there soon grew up a tradition of priestly intermediates who received the question, listened to the incoherent mumbling of the Oracle and prepared an appropriate reply, generally written out in verse.

In later times, the priests often came out with interpretations that suited their own purposes, sometimes with unhappy consequences for the inquirer. Even if they fulfilled their duties honestly, their utterances could be obscure.

Before their war with the Persians, for example, the Greek leaders went to Delphi to learn their prospects of success. They received a couplet: "Seedtime and harvest, weeping sires shall tell How thousands fought at Salamis and fell." It was less than helpful—although in the event it was the Greeks who won the seafight at Salamis. Another ruler on the eve of conflict was told: "You shall go you shall return never you shall perish in the war"—and was left to punctuate the perplexing message for himself.

Despite such frustrations, the oracles, especially that of Delphi, were deeply respected, serving as neutral points around which the creative tumult of Greek politics could revolve. When powerful citizens went to Delphi, reaching out to the divinities through the quirky and unreliable conduit opened by the Pythoness's holy trance, they left their pride behind; and even if the advice they received served them little, they learned humility from the experience.

Many seers held that the intentions of the gods could reach men and women more directly. With nightfall came sleep; with sleep came dreams. The science of oneiromancy—the interpretation of dreams—was old when the Pharaohs ruled in Egypt. Hieroglyphs on crumbling papyrus, inscribed by the dream-diviners of Egypt's Middle Kingdom, established some ground rules for students of the craft. "If a man sees

Wreathed in trance-inducing vapors and attended by sacred serpents, the oracles
of ancient Greece delivered messages from the gods. Warnings, promises and
prophecies were freely given, but cloaked in phrases of a tantalizing ambiguity.

himself in a dream looking at a snake: good. It signifies abundance of provision." But, "If a man sees in a dream his bed on fire: bad. It signifies the rape of his wife."

Many dreamers and diviners alike were convinced that helpful or informative dreams could be provoked by design, if the sleeper passed the night in an appropriate place. Greeks who visited the Oracle at Delphi often hoped for a message of their own during their stay, delivered in the form of a dream. The cult of Asclepius, Greece's god of healing, was founded on directed dreams, a process known as incubation. The hopeful sick made their way to the god's great shrine at Epidauros; with luck, as they slept in the temple dormitory, they would see the god come to them with a cure.

The Greeks differentiated between fanciful dreams—deceptions perpetrated

upon the sleeper by divine caprice—and dreams that were windows on the truth. Two gates, it was said, led from the world of shadows into the mind of the dreamer: a gate of ivory, which released only chimeras, and a gate of horn, through which emerged the accurate likenesses of things to come. It was through this second portal that a vision came to Penelope, wife of Odysseus, royal General of the Greek troops in the war with Troy. During her spouse's long absence, she was plagued by a horde of suitors demanding that she give herself in marriage.

She was, they insisted, a widow—for many years had passed without word from her lord. Daily they visited her, to drink deep from her wine barrels and feast on the rich provisions that the laws of hospitality demanded she supply. Making themselves at home in her house, they cajoled her, their lips moist with ill-suppressed lechery, their eyes straying to the jewels on her bosom and the fat flocks that grazed outside her door.

One day a stranger interrupted their revelry. He was as threadbare as any beggar, but his form and manner hinted of a higher birth. He claimed that he was an old acquaintance of Odysseus, a Prince from the island of Crete who had befriended the hero and given him shelter during his travels. Now he was himself a wanderer, and although he had no idea of Odysseus' whereabouts, he promised Penelope that her husband was alive and well. Warmed by these assurances, Penelope asked her guest to interpret a dream that had disturbed her. She kept a flock of twenty geese, as much for the pleasure in their company as for the pot. But in her dream, all twenty were attacked and killed by a giant eagle. Leaving its prey broken-necked upon the ground, it flew up to perch on a roofbeam and addressed Penelope in human speech. The geese, said the bird, were her would-be lovers, and the eagle itself Odysseus incognito, returned to claim his rightful place.

There was, responded the stranger, no ambiguity. What the eagle promised would come to pass. Penelope reminded her guest that the gods often sent false dreams through the gate of ivory. Only later, when the ragged visitor had slain his rivals and revealed himself as her long-lost spouse, would she accept that this prophecy had come to her through the truthful gate of horn.

Sages elsewhere believed that dreams were best interpreted in a sense quite

Penelope, wife to long-absent Odysseus, dreamed of a predator slaughtering her geese. A stranger interpreted the vision as a premonition of her husband's return, when he would slay the fortune-hunting suitors who assailed her.

opposite to their obvious meaning. Such was the premise of an old Indian treatise on dreams. Nightmares in which the dreamer had his limbs or genitals hacked off, it said, were omens of good fortune; conversely, to dream of playing with a lotus was a warning of the real-life amputation of an arm or leg. A man who dreamed that he was chained by iron would be sure to marry a virgin. The treatise's authors also noted that dreams that appeared early in the night were the last to be fulfilled, while those received shortly before the dawn were coming to pass even as the sleeper dreamed them.

But of all the schools of divination, none was so potent, nor so terrible, as the dark discipline that sought to pry the secrets of past and future from the sealed lips of the dead. Its practitioners were the necromancers, most fearless—and most feared—of all soothsayers.

Their method was powerful but perilous, and not to be used unless all else had failed. One of the earliest accounts of successful necromancy comes from the Old Testament, when King Saul of Israel, despairing at the strength of the Philistines, sent for a witchwoman out of Endor; she called up for him the spirit of the prophet Samuel, who promised the King success in battle. But the experience was painful: Saul "fell at once full length upon the ground, filled with fear."

The Roman historian Lucan told an even more harrowing tale of a summoning during the Civil Wars. Sextus Pompey, anticipating battle on the morrow with Caesar's host, asked the archwitch Erichtho for advice. She

A deck of cards embodied destiny. The hand a player drew could intimate disaster, joy or death.

was a fearful woman, who "never hesitated to commit murder, should the warm lifeblood from a slit throat be needed for her spells." But she agreed to help, provided a "clear-voiced recent corpse" could be found among the crop of dead from that day's skirmish. The witch selected a relatively undamaged cadaver, drained its veins and replenished them with warm menstrual blood mixed with "the froth of dogs suffering from hydrophobia, a lynx's guts, the hump of a corpse-eating hyena" and other extraordinary ingredients. And when Sextus and his retinue flinched in terror, she sneered, "Cowards, it is the dead who have reason to fear *me!*"

The wretched victim was duly made to speak. But for his pains, Sextus got little joy from the prophecy. "Tell your family not to shrink from death," said the dead man grimly; the next day Sextus' army was destroyed at Pharsalus.

Revenants from the realm of the dead, god-smitten oracles, dream apparitions—all these gave voice to their secrets. But out of the East, in the centuries of crusades and conflict, came another mysterious band of emissaries who had much to tell, yet kept silent. These entities, powerful in their knowledge and terrible in their reticence, were the figures painted in vivid colors upon a deck of cards: the symbols of the Tarot.

Whether enacted in the cell of a master magician or in the flimsy booth of a fairground Gypsy, the reading of the Tarot cards was a solemn ceremony. Unwrapped from the silk that protected

Thirteen was always a number of ill omen. Its evil reputation found vivid illustration in the Tarot pack, whose thirteenth card represented the Grim Reaper, Death.

its potency, the deck had to be shuffled by the hands of the questioner. Directed by the initiate, he or she then selected certain cards and laid them out in a pattern ritually prescribed, which the Tarot-reader would then interpret according to an age-old system.

There was a total of seventy-eight cards in most packs. The minor arcana, the "lesser mystery," contained fifty-six of them, divided into the cryptic suits of Batons, Cups, Swords and Coins. But the Tarot's real power lay in the major arcana, twenty-two cards each of a unique design, and each charged to groaning point with meaning and countermeaning. The Fool, the Magician, the Tower, the Hanged Man, the Chariot—even their names stirred ripples in the pool of mystery. Read by an intuitive practitioner,

the Tarot cards opened a new gateway to insight and prophecy.

The Hanged Man, for instance—a youth dangling inverted from a gallows tree, with one leg crossed behind the other and an expression of tranquil wisdom on his haloed features—could be taken to mean self-sacrifice. Yet a sensitive intelligence, following the card's symbolism through, would see the meaning open up like a flower at daybreak. The gallows was the Tree of Life; the knot that held the man suspended was Faith; the hanging itself stirred pagan echoes. Did not Odin, god of the dark north, hang nine days from a tree until the mystery of the runes was opened up to him? And what of the act of suspension between heaven and earth? To the adept, the reverberations were endless, the more so because many had trained by means of hours spent in a trance-state, immersing themselves in the subtleties of each symbolic card.

A French magician, Eliphas Levi, considered the Tarot as far more than an aid to divination. In its intricate design, he saw "the universal key of magical works," with whose aid he could "open the sepulchers of the ancient world, to make the dead speak, to behold the monuments of the past in all their splendor, to understand the enigmas of every sphinx and to penetrate all sanctuaries." In the major arcana's twenty-two cards, he found a link with the twenty-two letters of the Hebrew alphabet; in the four suits of the minor arcana he saw

not only the four elements but also the four letters of the Hebrew Tetragrammaton: the one true name of the one true God, which must never be pronounced.

Cunning fortunetellers could exploit the divinatory potential of ordinary playing cards as well as Tarot. The systems they employed differed from country to country and century to century, but they used the standard deck for prediction and character analysis. The four suits were thought to govern different human types and temperaments: Hearts were the sign of the fair-skinned, the amorous and the nobly born; Clubs of dark-skinned folk with a penchant for hard work and profitable deals; Diamonds governed the mild-mannered and penny-wise, while Spades ruled those grave-faced dignitaries who governed states and commanded armies.

A good deal of the cards' full meaning was found in their numbering. Each card in a suit bore a different message. The Four of Diamonds, for instance, foretold of a legacy, while the Nine in the same suit warned of a loss. But a number that was auspicious in one suit was not necessarily happy in another: In Hearts the ninth card promised a wish come true, while in Spades it spoke of suffering ahead. Simplistic as these signs might be, they had their underpinning—however corrupted or debased—in a completely separate branch of the secret arts, perhaps the purest of all, and certainly one of the most far-reaching: numerology.

Men and women had seen awesome significance in the shimmering clarity of numbers ever since they had learned to count. To those initiated into their mys-

terious workings, they were pure and abstract things, cleaner and infinitely more precise than the coarse, earthly quantities they were used to measure. Numbers could combine to form new numbers; the relationship between them could be expressed in yet more numbers. They could be manipulated with an exquisite, intellectual grace. Numbers, in short, were the nearest that mortals could reach to the crystalline perfection of divinity.

This fascination gripped thinkers in every civilization—and none more thoroughly than the Greek mystic and mathematician Pythagoras. His enlightenment, it was said, was the result of his study of music. He discovered the arithmetical ratios that governed octaves, fourths and fifths: 2:1, 3:2 and 4:3. But Pythagoras was not content to explain harmony by means of numbers. In a great conceptual leap, he understood that harmony *was* number, and number harmony.

Pythagoras and his followers pushed the gleaming new idea further, until they had proved to their satisfaction that "all things are number." From the concept of odd and even, they deduced the idea of limit and the unlimited; and they went on to proclaim a whole series of oppositions that extended the magical power of their beloved number. Male and female, rest and motion, light and darkness, good and evil: These and other dichotomies were encompassed and in a sense controlled by the art of these first numerologists.

Pythagoras also devoted much time to the establishment of a mysterious religion based on the transmigration of souls. Within a few generations, the faith had vanished, leaving behind it only a few baffling commandments such as: "To abstain from beans," "Not to touch a white cock," and "Not to walk on highways." But his numerical insights were the foundation of a new occult science. After his death, generations of numerologists polished and refined it, incorporating ideas with origins far removed in space and time from ancient Greece. Yet it continued to sparkle with the same glorious simplicity that had inspired Pythagoras.

Every number had its meaning, said the adept, and the number One was the pillar, stern and unique, upon which all the other meanings rested. It represented the divine principle, the good; it was sometimes regarded as masculine, the "father of numbers," and it conveyed the qualities of daring and self-reliance, stubbornness and austerity.

Two was One's opposite: the "mother of numbers," associated with boldness as well as strife. Christian numerologists assigned it to the devil; they also noted that, in the Bible, "God saw that it was good" after every day of creation except the second. But beneath Pythagoras' harmonic reasoning lay a dark magic that reached down to the taproot of humanity.

Pairs were always uncanny: The birth of twins was a great jolt to the natural order of the universe. Usually twins signaled danger and often they had to be slaughtered at birth. Sometimes they brought good fortune: Rome was founded by the twin brothers Romulus and Remus. And sometimes they became gods:

4	9	2
3	5	7
8	1	6

An arithmetical talisman

Wizards learned to make numbers work for them in the most ingenious ways. One of the most remarkable was the diagram known as a magic square—a chessboard-like arrangement of numbers selected so that every row and each diagonal in the grid added up to the same sum. According to the rules of numerology, each number could be used only once, and a true magic square had to include every consecutive number from one until the square was filled.

Creation of the squares could be a laborious process, far beyond the skill or patience of ordinary mortals. But for the adept, the result was well worth while: Magic squares had healing and talismanic powers, which varied according to the arrangement of numbers.

The small square shown above, in which each row and diagonal adds up to fifteen, was engraved on lead as an amulet. It helped ease the pains of childbirth and brought success in dealings with the mighty. But, like any powerful prescription, it had to be handled with great care. If it was worn on days when astrologers predicted an unfavorable aspect of the planet Saturn, it could hinder productive work and sow the seeds of discord.

From India to Scandinavia, twin gods were part of the pantheon, sometimes incarnate as the sun and the moon.

Two also produced the fearful idea of the double, the usually invisible duplicate of a person, whose appearance was almost always a warning of imminent death. Less supernatural duplicates, such as reflections in a mirror or a pool of water, or even shadows, also triggered the fear of pairing, and led to endless battles of charm and countercharm.

Three was called the "perfect number," the sum of the masculine and the feminine, containing within itself the beginning, the middle and the end. It marked the Christian Trinity, the past, present and future of time, and the three dimensions of space. It was a number of spirit and of completion, the first true masculine number. Four, on the other hand, was the number of matter: One is a point, Two yields a line and Three a plane surface, but Four grants solidity to the series. It was linked to earthly things, to toil and often to ill luck.

Five is the sum of Two and Three, of female and male; hence for a man it was the number of marriage. Midway between One and Nine, it was seen as ambivalent and lively, associated with the five senses. Six is the product of Two and Three, and therefore the marriage number of woman. It is mathematically perfect in a way that Three is not: 1 + 2 + 3 and 1 x 2 x 3. Hence it was the number of love, balanced and harmonious.

Seven was perhaps the most mystic of all numbers, a fusion of the spiritual Three and the earthly Four. There were seven "planets" known to ancient astrologers (the sun, moon, Mercury, Venus, Mars, Jupiter and Saturn), seven days of the week and seven days of creation. Its sacred and ritual attributes were legion.

To the Pythagoreans, Eight was the number of justice and fullness. Because it was twice Four, it was considered highly materialistic, though sometimes shouldering twice Four's burden of bad luck. Yet there are eight notes in a full chord, the Pythagorean measure for a man.

Nine stepped one beyond Eight and man, and achieved a new perfection. As the square of Three, it is a trinity of trinities, powerful and complete. It has a circular quality, in that multiplied by any other number, nine will yield itself again. Thus 5 x 9 = 45; 4 + 5 = 9.

Nine was also the highest number of the basic series, since generally in numerology Ten, Eleven, Twelve and all subsequent numbers are reduced to their simplest forms, Ten becoming One plus Zero and beginning the sequence anew. But some later numbers exercised power in their own right. Forty, for example, was for Pythagoreans a vital unit during pregnancy, which they believed required seven times forty days; in Babylon, it was esteemed as "the excellent quality," and the Bible, both Hebrew and Christian, is studded with references to spells of forty days and forty years.

The number that cast the longest shadow was always Thirteen. Pythagoras' system gave it no startling significance, but by Roman times it was already linked

The number three was inextricably linked with the ancient Greek goddess Hecate. She possessed three incarnations—mare, dog and lion—and three heads to see in all directions. Hecate ruled over the triad of human existence—birth, life and death—and the triple planes of the physical planet, the underworld, the earth and the air. Her dominions also embraced the tripartite temporal sphere of past, present and future. It was believed that the goddess drew her powers of enchantment from the moon, with its three phases, new, full and old.

The triple reins of power that she held over humanity, time and space made her an indispensable ally to the sorcerers who sought to work changes on the seemingly immutable physical world. Those brave enough to invoke her name in their spells were rewarded with a share of her uncanny powers.

to misfortune. Quite independently, it was an ill-starred number in the Norse tradition, too. Once, when twelve gods were feasting in Valholl, the evil spirit Loki joined them uninvited. By foul cunning, he caused the death of the beloved Balder, god of light. The final outcome was Ragnarök, the downfall of Valholl itself: Loki's Thirteen could hardly have been more catastrophic.

In Christian numerology, Thirteen was the number present at the Last Supper; it was the quorum for witches' covens; and in the Tarot it was the number of the grim card, Death. Always, Thirteen was shrouded in evil omen, so enveloped in doom that its legend fed itself without the need for further explanation.

In any case, most explanations of the power of numbers soon turned circular. Did Loki make Thirteen unlucky? Or did he simply make use of the number's innate malevolence as an ally in his evil scheme? The elegant systems of the numerologists allowed them access to the power and granted them certain rights of manipulation, but the power's source remained deeply hidden. Like an unknown planet circling in the darkness, it could be measured only by its pull.

Numerology's ambition and complexity reached its zenith in the work of the medieval Cabala—a marvelous system of metaphysical theology created originally by a fraternity of Jewish scholars. Sometimes working under threat of violent persecution and often the object of bewildered suspicion, they labored to interpret the Hebrew scriptures in the light of their vast knowledge of astrology and the occult. In ancient Hebrew, every letter had a numeric value as well as a literal one; the Cabalists—in a system they called the Gematria, the Hebrew version of the word geometry—sought to assign a number value to many of the key words in the sacred Hebrew texts. By searching out other words of the same value, they discovered mystical correspondences that had hitherto escaped notice.

The Cabalists' careful reduction of words to numbers did not originate with them; numerologists had always dabbled in the art, and since the Greek alphabet also uses letters as number signs, Pythagoras himself may have experimented with it. But no one before the Cabalists had pursued the task with such vigor, and their esoteric labors put prophetic analysis within the reach of anyone who could master basic arithmetic.

Wizards in the West adapted the code for their own languages and alphabets, assigning every letter a numerical equivalent. The so-called Chaldean alphabet gave every letter a value between one and eight. A, I, J, Q and Y counted as one; B, K and R as two; C, G, L and S were worth three; D, M and T, four; E, H, N and X, five; U, V and W equaled six; O and Z, seven; and F and P valued eight. And thus, by means of simple addition, any name could be reduced to one of the elementary numbers between one and nine. The arithmetical sum of any name's components was itself a symbol, revealing certain truths about the person, the city or even the nation that bore it. Scholars in many lands wrote texts to aid interpretation, but there were other adepts who preferred to keep their secret wisdom unwritten, locked behind their own sealed lips and communicated, when the time was ripe, to a younger magician judged worthy of the inheritance.

The most ambitious of the numerologists were not satisfied with merely the name-number of the object of their inquiries. They preferred to match it with other numbers, obtained from astrological calculations built around birthdates or Zodiacal signs. But the name was at the heart of the study; armed with it alone, a practitioner with a subtle knowledge of the shades of meaning could penetrate the secrets of the heart and map the unknown paths of human destiny.

For those scholars so gifted, the permutations were endless, the possibilities intoxicating. Obsessed, the students of such secrets burned their lamps while others slept, wandering in labyrinths of their own creation, in the place where mathematics and magic met.

Ghostly replicas presaging doom

Woe to any mortals who met their own fetch—an identical image of themselves that foretold death. Just where the double came from, no one knew for sure. Some people believed it was the immortal soul projected in bodily form. Others thought it entered the world at the moment of birth and passed away when the body died. Whatever the truth, it was known to congregate with others of its kind: At midnight on All Souls' Eve, the fetches of local people fated to die that year trooped into village churches.

Only the foolish ventured out to observe them at that hour, since they risked seeing themselves. If that happened, they could only commend their souls to heaven. A girl might swoon, a man might draw his sword, but nothing could protect the self-seer from the tomb.

The Esoteric Number

The number seven radiated power. No witch engendered more fear than she who was the seventh daughter of a seventh daughter, no physician healed more skillfully than he who was the seventh son of a seventh son. In prophecies, sevens appeared with uncanny regularity. Ancient seers, predicting the world's end, warned of seven seals that would be broken, seven plagues that would be suffered, seven trumpets that would be sounded before the destruction was complete.

The earliest sages, pondering the mysteries of space and time, looked skyward and counted seven planets, saw seven colors in the rainbow, studied the moon's mutations and observed that each of its four phases lasted for seven days at a time. Poets and priests told how, in the cosmic battle for mortal souls, the foul-visaged monsters of the seven deadly sins clashed against the angelic embodiments of the seven virtues. And every human lifespan encompassed seven ages, progressing from infancy to decrepitude.

For the old philosophers, every number was a symbol of a higher truth. Seven was the sum of three, the number of spiritual harmony, and four, representing earthly solidity. Yet no other numbers could be multiplied to make seven. It was solitary, pure and virginal, and therein lay its magic.

Pride

Wrath

Envy

Lust

Gluttony

Avarice

Sloth

Seven deadly sins, medieval reprobates were warned, preyed upon humankind and imperiled souls. Of the seven devils that tempted mortals to vice, Lucifer instilled pride, Mammon avarice and Beelzebub gluttony.

41

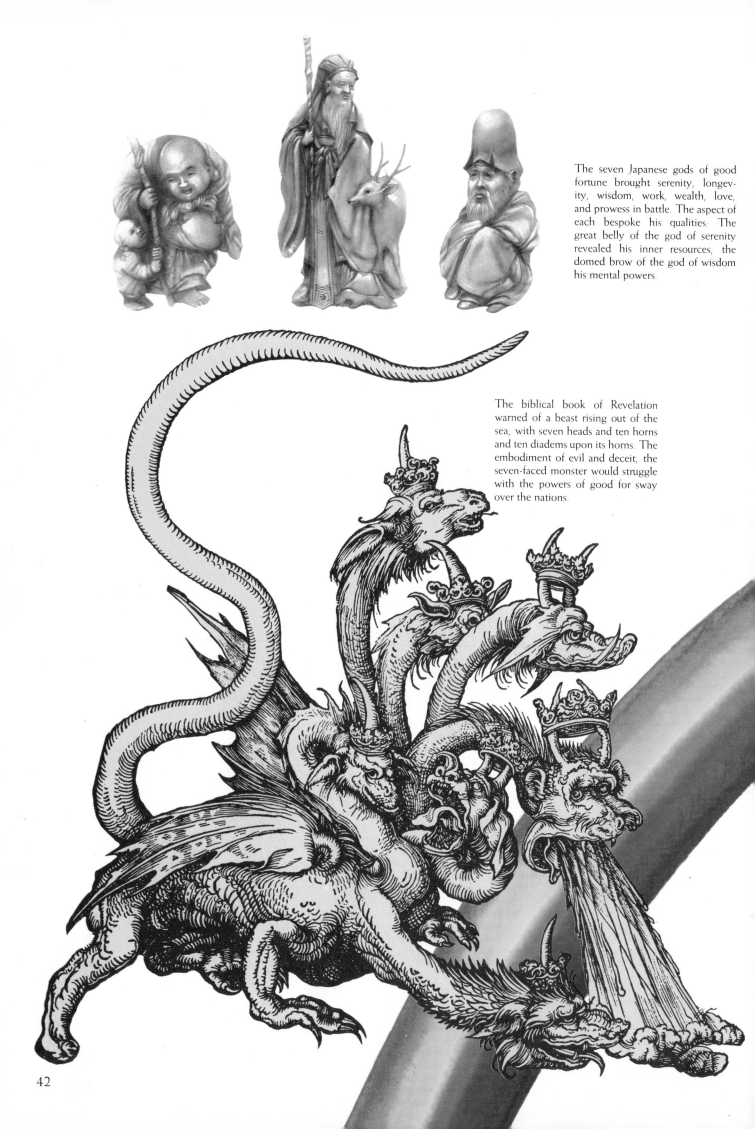

The seven Japanese gods of good fortune brought serenity, longevity, wisdom, work, wealth, love, and prowess in battle. The aspect of each bespoke his qualities: The great belly of the god of serenity revealed his inner resources, the domed brow of the god of wisdom his mental powers.

The biblical book of Revelation warned of a beast rising out of the sea, with seven heads and ten horns and ten diadems upon its horns. The embodiment of evil and deceit, the seven-faced monster would struggle with the powers of good for sway over the nations.

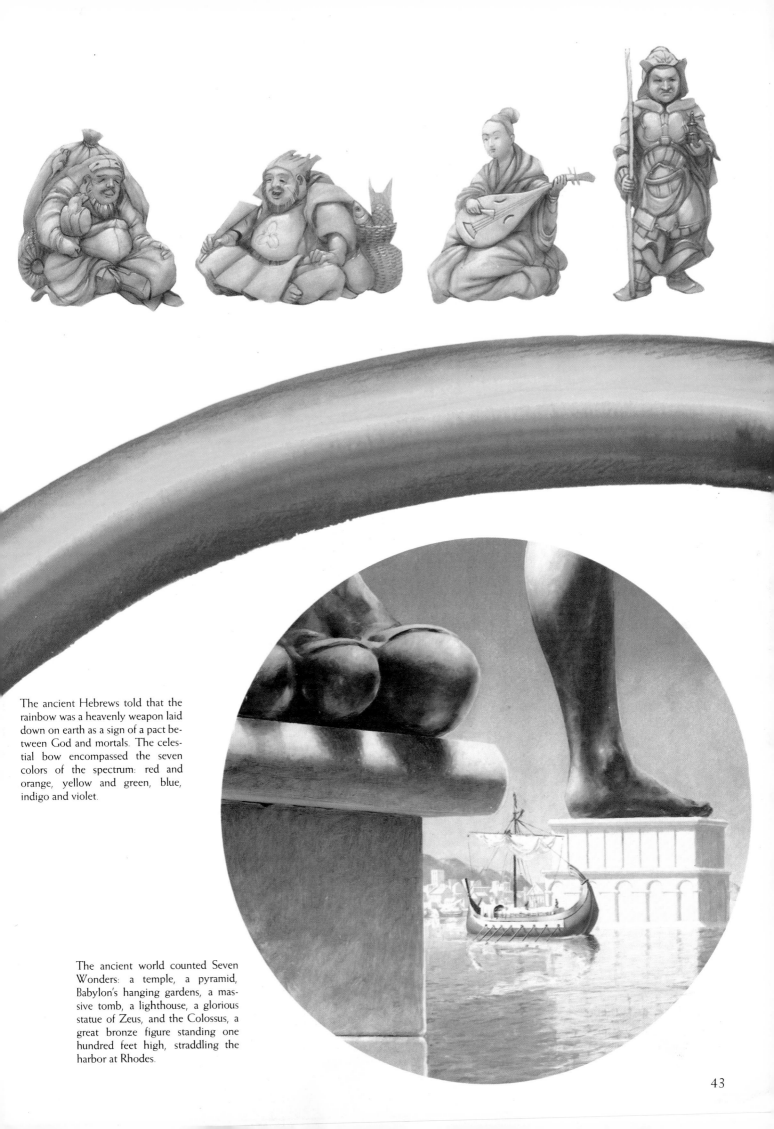

The ancient Hebrews told that the rainbow was a heavenly weapon laid down on earth as a sign of a pact between God and mortals. The celestial bow encompassed the seven colors of the spectrum: red and orange, yellow and green, blue, indigo and violet.

The ancient world counted Seven Wonders: a temple, a pyramid, Babylon's hanging gardens, a massive tomb, a lighthouse, a glorious statue of Zeus, and the Colossus, a great bronze figure standing one hundred feet high, straddling the harbor at Rhodes.

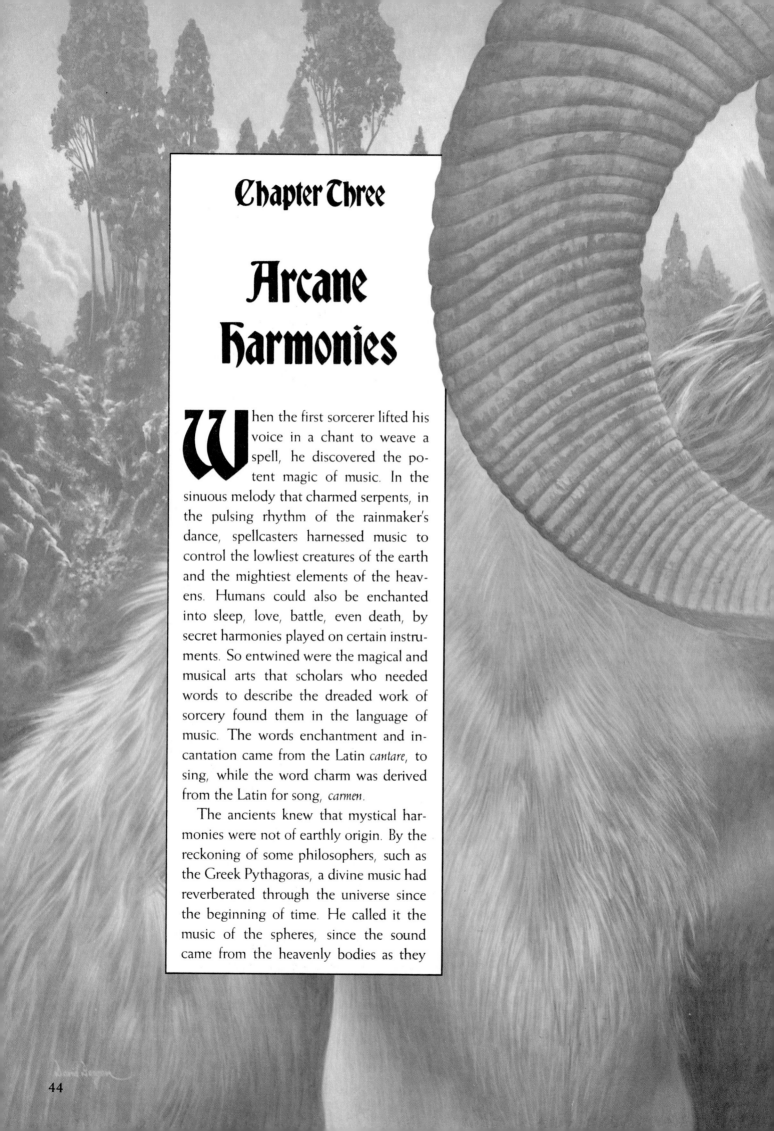

Chapter Three

Arcane Harmonies

When the first sorcerer lifted his voice in a chant to weave a spell, he discovered the potent magic of music. In the sinuous melody that charmed serpents, in the pulsing rhythm of the rainmaker's dance, spellcasters harnessed music to control the lowliest creatures of the earth and the mightiest elements of the heavens. Humans could also be enchanted into sleep, love, battle, even death, by secret harmonies played on certain instruments. So entwined were the magical and musical arts that scholars who needed words to describe the dreaded work of sorcery found them in the language of music. The words enchantment and incantation came from the Latin *cantare*, to sing, while the word charm was derived from the Latin for song, *carmen*.

The ancients knew that mystical harmonies were not of earthly origin. By the reckoning of some philosophers, such as the Greek Pythagoras, a divine music had reverberated through the universe since the beginning of time. He called it the music of the spheres, since the sound came from the heavenly bodies as they

Collusions of sweet sounds and savagery

In the days when wolves roamed the forests of France, many tales were told of men who possessed a sinister rapport with the beasts. Music, it was said, could charm them into submission, and every flautist was suspected of an evil association with a ravening pack. Rumor held that some musicians were not true men at all, but were werewolves, who at the stroke of midnight acquired the fangs and bristling pelt of their fawning confreres.

Summoning his savage associates to a forest glade with a haunting note, a minstrel would charm them with the sound of his flute or bagpipes. Once the animals were spellbound, they became as obedient as dogs. If the sorcerer-musician bore any man a grudge, he would murmur to the wolves the whereabouts of his enemy's flocks. Their bloodlust aroused, the wolves and their leader would dance, howling, around a blazing fire, then set off to wreak havoc. After such a night, the morning would discover a field strewn with the bloody carcasses of slain lambs and ewes. Meanwhile, the leader of the wolves walked again among men, his crime suspected but impossible to prove.

whirled through the cosmos. The seven visible planets corresponded to the seven notes of the musical scale, and with these seven notes the heavens sang. Mortals were deaf to this celestial music only because they had never known its absence. Should it cease, mankind would realize what perfection had been lost.

Among the immortals were many musicians, such as Pan, who cut the first pipes from a bundle of reeds, and Apollo, who played the first lyre. When the gods feasted, Apollo played for them while the nine Muses supplied an antiphonal chorus. Divine patrons of all the arts, the Muses sang with such enchantment that even the great Zeus looked upon them with favor.

Among humankind, those who could count gods among their ancestors were often blessed with the divine gift of music. One such hero was the Finnish patriarch Vainamöinen, who had been begotten of a goddess by the wind and the waves. Wise and white-haired from birth, he was a natural leader of younger men. Once, he set sail in the company of men and women across the wide, icy waters of a lake called Pohja. Their craft was heavy-laden with food and weapons, tents and horses, so Vainamöinen steered carefully. Yet the boat suddenly pitched, shuddered and stopped dead in the water, flinging everyone onto the deck. As they got to their feet, a boisterous youth named Lemminkäinen lifted up the rudder from the stern. His friend Ilmarinen pulled a spar from the rigging. Prodding

beneath the water with their makeshift poles they felt something under the boat, something harder than a sandbar, yet more yielding than a rock. Peering into the waves, Lemminkäinen saw a shadowy gray shape beneath them. It was larger than the boat itself and, with sluggish twists and turns, it was moving.

Lemminkäinen staggered back from the side of the vessel. They were caught not on rocks or tree branches, he cried, but on the shoulders of an enormous pike. Calmly, old Vainamöinen told him to cut the fish in half with his sword.

Eager to show his prowess, the youth thrust his blade into the water, but its weight was great and he fell in after it. Laughing, Ilmarinen reached down and caught his friend by the hair. He dragged him up into the boat, then hefted his own sword and plunged it into the pike's back. With a ripple of its powerful muscles, the mighty fish broke the blade.

Undeterred by sword thrusts, a giant pike
rose from the frigid waters of a Finnish lake
to menace a boat-load of sages and heroes.

47

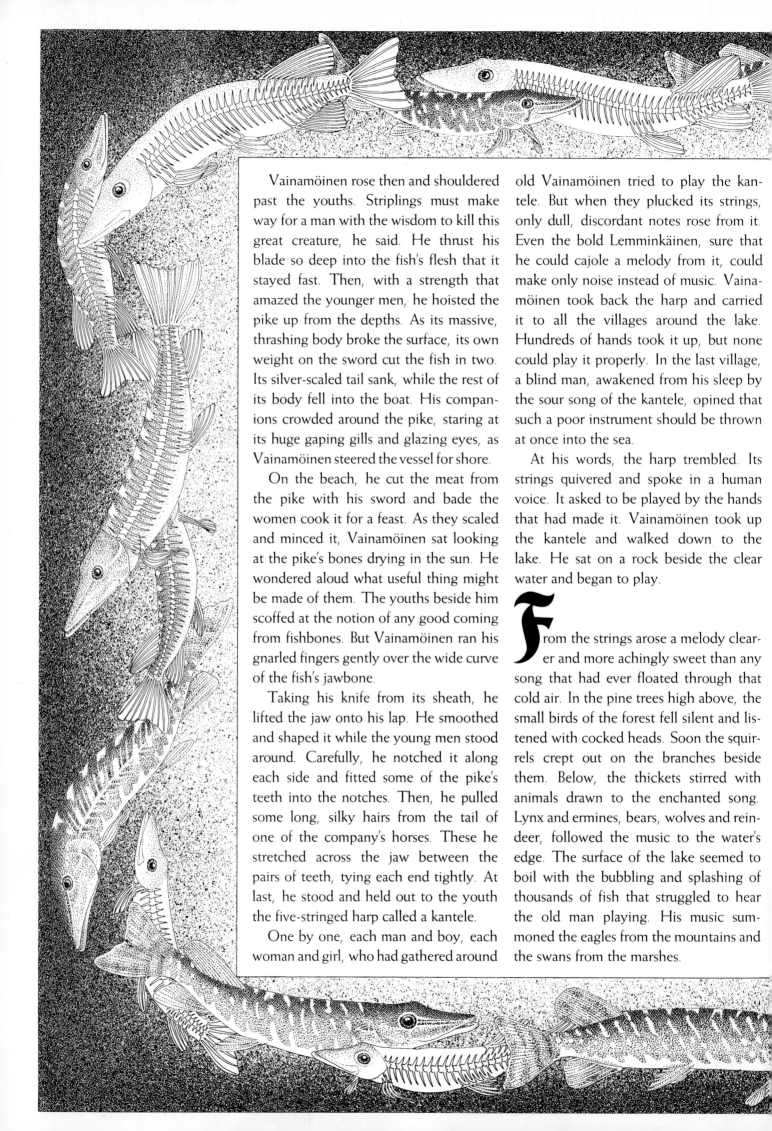

Vainamöinen rose then and shouldered past the youths. Striplings must make way for a man with the wisdom to kill this great creature, he said. He thrust his blade so deep into the fish's flesh that it stayed fast. Then, with a strength that amazed the younger men, he hoisted the pike up from the depths. As its massive, thrashing body broke the surface, its own weight on the sword cut the fish in two. Its silver-scaled tail sank, while the rest of its body fell into the boat. His companions crowded around the pike, staring at its huge gaping gills and glazing eyes, as Vainamöinen steered the vessel for shore.

On the beach, he cut the meat from the pike with his sword and bade the women cook it for a feast. As they scaled and minced it, Vainamöinen sat looking at the pike's bones drying in the sun. He wondered aloud what useful thing might be made of them. The youths beside him scoffed at the notion of any good coming from fishbones. But Vainamöinen ran his gnarled fingers gently over the wide curve of the fish's jawbone.

Taking his knife from its sheath, he lifted the jaw onto his lap. He smoothed and shaped it while the young men stood around. Carefully, he notched it along each side and fitted some of the pike's teeth into the notches. Then, he pulled some long, silky hairs from the tail of one of the company's horses. These he stretched across the jaw between the pairs of teeth, tying each end tightly. At last, he stood and held out to the youth the five-stringed harp called a kantele.

One by one, each man and boy, each woman and girl, who had gathered around old Vainamöinen tried to play the kantele. But when they plucked its strings, only dull, discordant notes rose from it. Even the bold Lemminkäinen, sure that he could cajole a melody from it, could make only noise instead of music. Vainamöinen took back the harp and carried it to all the villages around the lake. Hundreds of hands took it up, but none could play it properly. In the last village, a blind man, awakened from his sleep by the sour song of the kantele, opined that such a poor instrument should be thrown at once into the sea.

At his words, the harp trembled. Its strings quivered and spoke in a human voice. It asked to be played by the hands that had made it. Vainamöinen took up the kantele and walked down to the lake. He sat on a rock beside the clear water and began to play.

From the strings arose a melody clearer and more achingly sweet than any song that had ever floated through that cold air. In the pine trees high above, the small birds of the forest fell silent and listened with cocked heads. Soon the squirrels crept out on the branches beside them. Below, the thickets stirred with animals drawn to the enchanted song. Lynx and ermines, bears, wolves and reindeer, followed the music to the water's edge. The surface of the lake seemed to boil with the bubbling and splashing of thousands of fish that struggled to hear the old man playing. His music summoned the eagles from the mountains and the swans from the marshes.

Where the music touched human ears, men and women left their work and children abandoned their games. Everyone gathered amid the birds and animals. As the song reached its crescendo, even the gods of forest, water and sky appeared among the mortals to listen. All who heard the melody wept at its beauty. But the one whose eyes filled the fastest was Vainamöinen himself. As he played, his tears rolled slowly down onto the rocks and into the water.

Sensing that it was no common brine that he was weeping, Vainamöinen called out to all the company and asked for someone to retrieve his tears from the water's depths. The beasts were silent. The humans whispered to each other that no one could bring them back.

Again, the old man called for his tears, this time to a raven circling above him. Plummeting to the lake, the bird disappeared in the water. He was not a swimmer, though, and soon sputtered up to the surface. Then, a blue duck swooped down from the sky. It dived gracefully into the waves and knifed through the icy water, drawn toward a silvery gleam amid the black ooze of the lake bed.

On the beach, the crowd watched the waves in silence. Suddenly, the blue duck broke the surface and bobbed to the shore. Waddling up to Vainamöinen, it dropped a clutch of perfect white pearls at his feet. Like the tears they had been, the pearls shimmered in the sun with the last magic of the kantele's song.

The kantele accompanied Vainamöinen on his adventures until one fateful day when he was traversing a lake and a great storm swept the instrument into the dark waters. Vainamöinen was heartbroken but his vocation for music endured. In time, he fashioned another kantele from a birch and with it entranced the beasts, the trees, and the sun and moon themselves. Long after Vainamöinen's death, people remembered his haunting melodies as vividly as his heroic exploits.

While noble Vainamöinen had been a just recipient of the magical gift of music, unworthy souls were sometimes granted it too. A story was told in the mountains of Wales of an old cottager named Morgan who received an instrument from the fairies. One night, as Morgan nodded drowsily by his hearth, a knock on his door roused him. At his shouted welcome, three road-weary strangers entered the dwelling and asked for food. The graybeard, warmed by his fire, his pipe and his good ale, waved them toward the bread and cheese laid out on his table.

The travelers took what they needed, promising in return to grant any wish that Morgan had. He laughed at their nonsense and asked for a harp that would sing even for his stiff, clumsy fingers. Instantly, the strangers vanished. In their place stood a beautiful harp, so delicately wrought that only the smallest hands could have made it. Morgan recognized it as a fairy's instrument, just as—too late—he realized that his visitors had been fairies in human guise. He stared at the harp for a long while, wishing that he had asked for something better.

With an instrument wrought from the great pike's jaws, the wizard
Vainamöinen played the world's sweetest music. All the creatures
of the air, the flood and the forest came in peace to hear the melody.

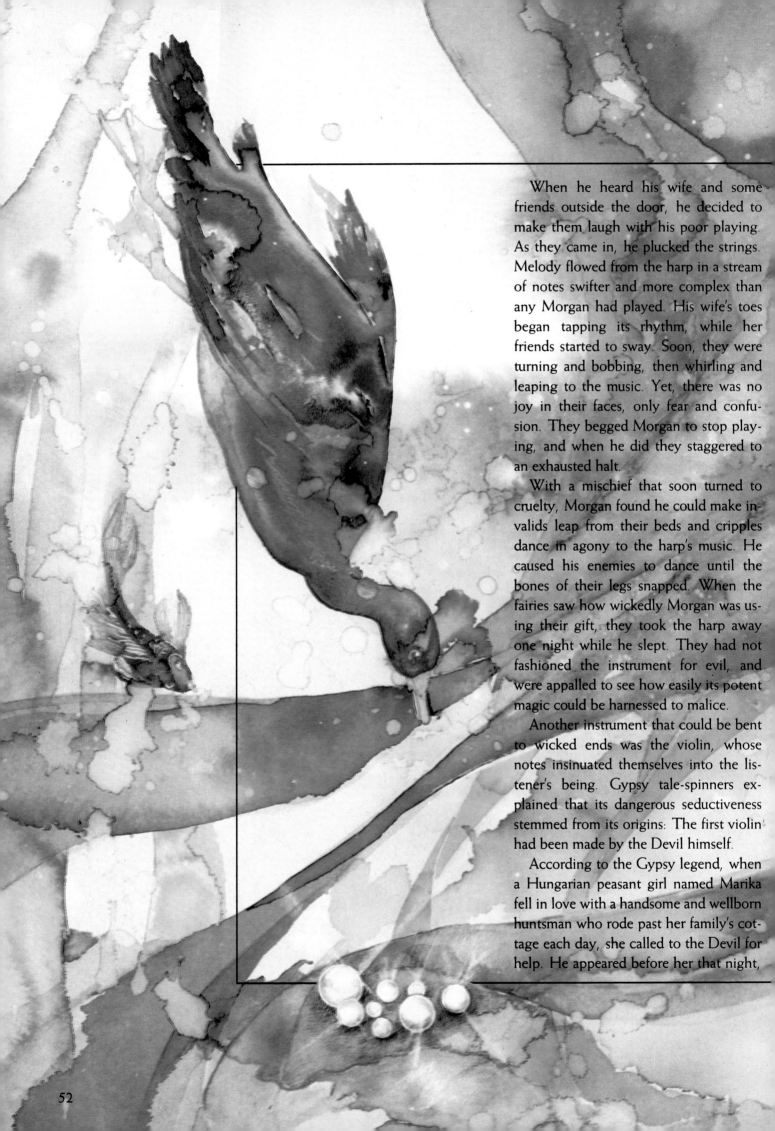

When he heard his wife and some friends outside the door, he decided to make them laugh with his poor playing. As they came in, he plucked the strings. Melody flowed from the harp in a stream of notes swifter and more complex than any Morgan had played. His wife's toes began tapping its rhythm, while her friends started to sway. Soon, they were turning and bobbing, then whirling and leaping to the music. Yet, there was no joy in their faces, only fear and confusion. They begged Morgan to stop playing, and when he did they staggered to an exhausted halt.

With a mischief that soon turned to cruelty, Morgan found he could make invalids leap from their beds and cripples dance in agony to the harp's music. He caused his enemies to dance until the bones of their legs snapped. When the fairies saw how wickedly Morgan was using their gift, they took the harp away one night while he slept. They had not fashioned the instrument for evil, and were appalled to see how easily its potent magic could be harnessed to malice.

Another instrument that could be bent to wicked ends was the violin, whose notes insinuated themselves into the listener's being. Gypsy tale-spinners explained that its dangerous seductiveness stemmed from its origins: The first violin had been made by the Devil himself.

According to the Gypsy legend, when a Hungarian peasant girl named Marika fell in love with a handsome and wellborn huntsman who rode past her family's cottage each day, she called to the Devil for help. He appeared before her that night, ready to grant any request if the girl could pay his price. He could give her the huntsman's love if she would give her four young brothers into his infernal keeping.

As the girl went from bed to bed in the cottage, gazing down at the sleeping figures, the Devil followed her. He looked at the boys greedily, but the girl's expression was distant, fixed on the beautiful huntsman in her mind's eye. She nodded to the Devil, who instantly transformed the boys into four lengths of string.

Next, he must have their father, her benefactor said. After the briefest pause, the girl agreed and watched as he changed the old man into a box that stretched from a rounded body to a long elegant neck. He fastened the strings across it and plucked them with his clawed fingers. At their twanging sound, the Devil looked pained and turned to the girl again.

He asked for her mother. Almost feeling the huntsman's embrace, Marika gestured to where the last of her family slept. From the old woman, the Devil fashioned a slender stick of wood strung on one side with a twist of her hair.

At last, the Devil drew the bow across the strings of the violin. Marika listened with wonder to music that trembled on the air like a human voice. In its song she seemed to hear her brothers' laughter, her mother's scolding, her father's prayers. As she began to weep, the Devil struck up a merry tune that transformed her mood to joy. Then he gave it to her, saying that its music would ensnare the huntsman's heart.

She played the violin in the forest the next day. As the huntsman rode by, he heard its haunting voice, heard in it all he had ever loved or dreamed of loving. He galloped up through the trees, joyously lifted the girl to his saddle and turned his horse toward home.

After only a few days, the Devil came looking for them. They had listened to his music and were his creatures now, he said, sweeping them away to hell. As Marika vanished in the infernal darkness, the violin slipped from her grasp and fell to the forest floor. There it lay with silent strings until a Gypsy boy found it among the leaves. Marveling at its lovely design, he plucked at it and tapped it with the bow. When at last he discovered how to draw the bow across the strings, he made a music Gypsies played ever afterward to make men laugh or weep.

In the hands of some spellcasters, music was a force to fight evil rather than to promote it. The delicate harmonies of certain stringed instruments, for example, were known to soothe the restless evil in creatures of the night. The Celtic musician Cailte used the enchantment of his lute against three werewolves that had ravaged the flocks of his countrymen. Early one morning, he climbed to the peak of a steep cairn and began to play. A lyrical melody floated down over forest and meadow, filling every hollow and glade and penetrating the deepest caves, where evil creatures hid from the sun.

Cailte played through all the hours of the morning and the afternoon. As evening drew on and the sun began to set, he saw three shapes darker than the dusk

A demon army put to flight

One musician skilled at taming malevolence with melody was Lady Pengerswick, an Eastern Princess who was married to a great Cornish enchanter. Lord Pengerswick had wed her during his sojourn among the magicians of the Orient, with whom he had studied the mystical arts. When he returned to Cornwall, he was a master of all the magical sciences save one: He could not bend a song to his will and make it work enchantment for him.

His bride possessed the very skill that her husband lacked. When Lord Pengerswick brought her to his castle in that cold, wet land so far from her home, she sang the songs of her childhood and accompanied herself with a harp's haunting harmonies. The words of her refrains were in a language not even her husband could understand. Her voice was low and sweet, yet it seemed to fill every room of the castle. The servants paused in their work to listen and mermaids gathered in the

cove below to catch the melody.

One night, while her strains floated through the castle, her husband resolved to put his prowess as a sorcerer to the test. With a potent incantation, he summoned the most unruly of evil spirits to visit him and bow to his magic.

They emerged from an oblivion darker than Lord Pengerswick had ever imagined. Hissing and spitting sulfurously, the hellborn company materialized around the frightened man. They whirled about him until he, too, was whirling and staggering. He shouted charms to dispel them, but in vain: The demons' unleashed fury was more powerful than the spoken word.

All seemed lost for the foolhardy wizard until, above the demons' snarls and his own cries, he heard the music of his wife's harp. The demons heard it, too, and their wild spinning slowed to the harp's gentle rhythm. The ordered harmony of her playing imposed itself on their chaos, lulling them into quietude. At last she sent them in the thrall of her music out through the air and back into the night.

the accompaniment of the charmed mody, the Sybarite army was routed.

God-fearing peasants and powerful socerers alike had always known the grenchantment in the sudden clash of gonor cymbals, the insistent beat of druand the solemn tolling of bells. Througthese percussive voices, mortals seemable to speak to ghosts or spirits, callithem up or driving them away.

In ancient Rome, sorcerers knew tsecret of casting a special bell that wburied along with a dead body for sevdays. If the bell were exhumed and ruron the eighth day, the corpse itself courise with the music. Roman householdewho wished to send family ghosts bacto the grave did so with a clash of cyrbals and the invocation: "Ghosts of nfathers, go forth!"

Both drums and bells were known
thwart storms, while the power of chimeto ward off evil was such that Westerexorcists traditionally rang bells whecasting out demons. In the East, Chines

*The bells of medieval churches tolled not only to announce a death
but to keep at bay the evil spirits that swarmed around the departed.*

priests struck gongs to drive spirits away. And at the precise moment of death, when the soul was most vulnerable to mystical influence, European church bells were rung to keep evil at bay.

During great festivals of the witch's calendar, such as Midsummer Eve and Walpurgis Night, the malevolence afoot was so terrible that some parishioners tolled church bells from dusk to dawn. The righteous power of bells often came from the saints to whom they were consecrated. Most well-loved bells were named—some were even baptized.

The mystical voices of such bells were nearly impossible to silence. Many centuries ago in England, an entire village was buried in an earthquake, but the chimes of the entombed church bell still rang each Christmas Eve. On the same night every year in one German town, three silver bells tolled from the bottom of a lake where they had fallen from a burning church steeple.

One of the most beloved bells in medieval times belonged to the church of St. Illtyd, in Wales. When an English King heard its sweet song on his travels, he stole it from its belfry and rode home with

it swinging from his horse's neck. Later, repenting of his crime, the King decided to return the bell to St. Illtyd's. But no sooner had he lashed it to his horse's neck once more than the animal galloped away, riderless, toward Wales.

The magical bell rang as the horse crossed the countryside of England, marking every stride of the westward journey. Other horses, hearing the wondrous music, fell under its enchantment. Leaping over walls and fences, they followed the bell westward. By the time the belled steed reached the Severn River at the Welsh border, a great bevy of horses followed behind him. The animals did not break stride at the river's edge, but galloped straight across the water, upheld by the music of the bell. On the other side more beasts joined them, until all the horses of Wales escorted the bell to the gate of St. Illtyd's church.

There, the King's steed lowered its head and allowed the priest to lift the charmed burden from its neck. Raised to the steeple, the bell rang out in a benison that released the horses from their spell. For centuries to come, the villagers listening to their bell blessed the horse that had sensed the mystical power of music and responded to its elusive magic.

Chapter Four

The Witch's Kitchen

In villages that clung to the storm-carved cliffs of Cornwall, mothers taught their daughters the lore of plants and flowers just as they taught them to churn fresh butter from thick cream. In their warm, firelit kitchens, hung with bundles of herbs to keep the plague away, the air was heavy with the scented steam of soothing infusions. Ointments to heal wounds and teas to tame fevers crowded their shelves, and hidden among them were amulets filled with more potent concoctions. These the good wives of the hamlet of Fraddam hung around their necks on market day, when the road to town took them past one cottage set apart from the rest.

The tumbledown house seemed almost part of the hedgerow; thorny branches wove themselves into its thatch, and ancient roots curled around its threshold. The women hurried past it, their faces averted, though there was little sign of life within. But sometimes, when the tides ran high and the moon was full, a greasy black smoke poured from its chimney. Enveloped by its stench, the women caught their children up in their arms and ran. The whisper would pass from cottage to cottage: The witch of Fraddam was in her kitchen.

The noxious fumes oozed up from the kitchen more frequently with each year that passed, for the district around Fraddam had become a battleground of magic where the witch's hellborn powers clashed with the more beneficent sorcery of a wizard who lived close by. Each time the crone bewitched herself into the farmer's churn and drank his milk, the wizard responded by burning her tongue with a hot poker. When she disfigured one of the village children with her evil eye, he restored it with a spell. Where she spread sickness, he cured it.

The witch wandered the countryside at night, gathering herbs by moonlight and listening at cottage windows for quarrels that might profit her in her spell-making. Against the midnight sky she could often see a single candle burning in the turret window of the wizard's home. There, she knew, her rival sat turning the brittle pages of books bound in ivory and edged with gold. The witch herself had passed her hands over such tomes, hoping to draw their powers, but no magic had come from them.

She turned from the light and spit, telling herself that she did not require spells from books. She made her own magic, just as her mother and grandmother had taught her, from herbs and flowers, cats' blood and toads' skin.

Yet her powers needed strengthening against the encroachments of her highborn and learned rival, and one moonlit night she climbed down the rocky cliffs above Kynance Cove to summon an ally. As the tide ran out, she kneeled at the water's edge and softly whispered a demon's name into the night.

Instantly, a hissing creature burst into being at her feet, its twisted, puckered face glowing red in the firelight. She crouched beside it and offered a bargain. The witch promised her soul in exchange for power over her enemy. But, as her tarnished soul was not a very great prize, the hellish creature refused her terms. Instead, it offered only the secret of a brew that would enslave anyone it touched.

Thinking the potion would be sufficient for her ends, the witch accepted the demon's offer and hurried home. In her smoke-stained kitchen, she mixed the ingredients of the infernal beverage in a caldron. Then she concocted a second preparation, a toxic dilution of deadly nightshade, in a bucket.

The next night, bent beneath the weight of her dual load, she trudged through the twisting lanes until she came to a crossroads she knew the wizard must pass. She placed the bucket in the middle of the road, where its poisoned water might tempt a hot, tired horse.

Keeping the caldron close beside her, the witch huddled down in a ditch and chuckled at the cleverness of her plan. The wizard's mare would drink deeply of the maddening tincture, and before her master could feel the witch's snare closing about him, he would be thrown by the crazed animal. It would be easy to douse

Waiting at a crossroads for the wizard who had thwarted her, the vengeful witch of Fraddam chuckled and stirred a hellish brew.

him with the caldron's contents as he lay stunned and helpless on the ground.

Hoofbeats drummed along the lonely road and the witch sank deeper into the shadows. Startled by the strange object at the crossroads, the mare reared. But the wizard's prescience was too great for the old woman. Leaning forward in his saddle, he whispered in the horse's ear. Instantly, the beast turned and kicked the bucket, which flew across the road and struck the caldron at the witch's feet. The crone screamed as the brew splashed over her.

The wizard shouted at the night sky, and a whirlwind came sweeping out of the still heavens. Riding on the crest of the storm was the demon from Kynance Cove, lashing it to greater fury. As the winds engulfed the witch, the bucket was sucked into the eye of the cyclone and stretched by magic into the shape of a coffin. The flying sarcophagus dipped earthward and scooped the crone up into the air. Her caldron bobbed up after her as she drifted out of sight. With a triumphant laugh, the wizard spurred his horse homeward. That night, and in all the nights to come when storms beat against the coast, he knew that the witch was still aloft on the wind, sometimes swooping down to stir up the sea beneath her. From the roof of his turret he had only to shout a word of command to watch the storm die away as his defeated rival deferred to his superior force.

The powers of both witch and wizard came not only from the demon's brew, but from an ancient knowledge of the plants that flowered in hedgerows, meadows and in graveyards. The men and women who wielded magic knew the properties of every growing thing, and how to bend them to their will.

The skill and cunning with which they manipulated nature was a legacy

from a long line of sorcerers stretching back across the centuries to the priests and priestesses of Hecate, in ancient Greece. Hecate, goddess of witchcraft, was embodied by the moon. Her suppliants knew that when its full orb hung cold and white in the night sky, the goddess's influence flowed down in its light upon all earthly life. Herbs picked under Hecate's spell would flavor any charm with superhuman malevolence.

Thus, the witch of Fraddam obeyed an age-old principle of her kind when she carried out her deadly harvest under the full moon. She and her rival practitioners worked by a complex calendar of days and hours to gather plants either for good or for ill. This magical timetable took account both of natural events, such as the passing seasons, and of the offices of the Church, whose festivals and holy days marked currents of particularly powerful spiritual influence to be exploited. When the witch desired to stir a quarrel between lovers in Fraddam, she picked vervain by the dawn light of a May morning to strew in their path. If she needed a charm to open locked doors, she waited until St. James's Day in high summer. Leaves of chicory cut with a golden blade at noon and again at midnight on that day were the essence of the spell. The old teachings decreed that betony must be gathered on May Day. During its harvest, an invocation of the Holy Trinity made the herb a healing simple, while a call to Satan ripened it for evildoing.

Most plants in the sorcerer's pharmacopoeia had a similar potential for either good or evil. Only a lifetime of careful study enabled the magician to handle them properly for the desired result. The

Foiled by a stronger magic, the witch was condemned forever to ride the clouds and the waves, raising storms in her wake.

out the devil, angelica was a potent ingredient against evil and danger. If it was picked, in accordance with ancient teachings, when the sun was in Leo, even a small piece of angelica could drive away pestilence and storms.

Rosemary, too, an ingredient in countless protective amulets, was a benevolent herb with the power to protect against both bodily and spiritual harm. So great was its innate virtue that only righteous people could cultivate it. A single sprig of the pine-scented herb would guard the wearer against evil spirits by day as well as against their nocturnal visitations in the guise of nightmares. Any man who feared that a poisoner might sit among his guests at the dinner table was wise to eat with a spoon carved from a rosemary bush, whose wood could purify tainted food. Many herbs and flowers could shield the virtuous against the infernal mischief of witches and fairies. Farmers and shepherds gained special protection from peonies, flowers thought by the ancient Greeks to ward off night spirits by shining in the dark. Cowherds garlanded the horns of their cattle with marsh marigolds

to keep enchantment at bay, while parents hung daisy chains around their children's necks lest fairy kidnappers should leave changelings in their beds.

Not all plants were benign. Some could be used to enhance, rather than guard against, witchcraft. It was said that parsley would flourish only in the gardens of evildoers. Even there it was slow to sprout: Its roots descended nine times to the underworld before sending up shoots replete with the devil's own malevolence. The malign influence of the herb basil was so potent that its leaves exuded a deadly miasma. The fern, too, was a useful aid to the magician. Cursed by Saint Patrick, it could bear no flowers; instead, it carried tiny seeds with the power to make a skillful sorcerer invisible.

Such herbs on their own, however, had relatively little power. For their most potent magic, spellmakers bolstered the plants' efficacy with the aid of other ingredients from the witch's kitchen. The blood, bone or skin of an animal often lent power to the concoction. In the trial of one sorcerer brought to justice by frightened townsfolk, the evidence included his witch's bag containing bears' claws, cats' ears, hedgehogs' bristles, the teeth of a mole and the bones of a mouse. Some of the most powerful unguents and ointments called for ingredients from the grave—human blood, brains and flesh. Because the stain of sin added to their efficacy, these ingredients were sought from unbaptized babies, still bearing the guilt of Adam's fall, and from hanged felons. Witches sought out lonely country gibbets and untended cribs for their grisly needs.

Fat taken from a felon's corpse had many magical uses. By long boiling, a witch could render it into tallow. Candles molded from this infernal wax had the power to disclose hidden treasure.

In the pharmacopoeia of sorcery were many embrocations that worked their magic on the human eye, the window of the soul. Since time began, the earth had been inhabited by more creatures than the mortal eye could see, but certain very secret salves sharpened human sight and allowed it to glimpse the realm of enchantment. One girl who unwittingly saw into that kingdom was young Cherry of Zennor, in Cornwall.

Cherry's father was a fisherman whose only wealth was his flock of handsome children. Cherry was the youngest, a beautiful child who ran barefoot on the beach in dresses her sisters had outgrown. When she was old enough to notice that other girls had new dresses and ribbons for their hair, she grew dissatisfied with the simple pleasures of her father's cottage by the sea. Her mother begged her to stay among the fisherfolk she knew, but proud Cherry was determined to find a life among the prosperous farmers who had beef for supper instead of periwinkles.

With no possessions to burden her, she simply set off one morning up the rising ground known as the Lady Downs. At first her step was light and quick, but after many hours and many miles she grew weary of walking and stopped to rest at a crossroads. The downland spread out around her, wide fields and empty roads as far as she could see. She had just closed her eyes when a voice spoke to her out of the emptiness. Cherry jumped to her feet. Looking down at her with kindly eyes was a man—a gentleman, Cherry knew, by the gleaming leather of his boots and the fine wool of his cloak. She curtsied in respectful silence, though she was longing to ask how he had come upon her so unexpectedly.

The gentleman asked where Cherry was going, and when she told him he smiled. He had gone out that very day to find a girl to keep house for him; he was a widower whose young son needed tending. Cherry's chores would be simple in his comfortable house with its warm fires and richly stocked larder. As he spoke, the girl nodded and said "Yes, sir" as her mother had taught her to say to gentlemen. Soon she found herself accompanying him. They walked and walked, yet Cherry still felt fresh when they stopped before a gate in a high stone wall.

Together, they stepped through the gate into a garden lovelier than any Cherry had seen or imagined. Flowers of every color blossomed at her feet like a silken carpet. Against the garden wall, espaliered fruit trees spread branches that were heavy with ripe apples, pears and plums. The plants in this garden seemed to know no season; the fruits and flowers of spring grew beside those of summer and autumn, all ready to be picked.

Night-roving hags wandered the highways in search of gibbets and their human burdens, for the flesh of hanged men was a sovereign ingredient in maleficent spells.

The gentleman—her master now—held open the door of his manor house for Cherry, who blushed at his courtesy. Inside the handsome hall, he called his son. The boy was no more than three years old, yet he met Cherry's friendly smile with a cold, piercing gaze.

The man described her new life, its easy duties and ready pleasures. She would sleep in the child's room, cook and care for him by day and tend the garden while he played. The rules were few, her master said, but strict. Never must she open her eyes at night. Never could she stray into the many rooms whose doors were always closed. Most importantly, each morning she must bathe the boy's eyes with an ointment, but never let it touch her own.

Cherry took up her work the next day. She bathed the boy in a spring at the bottom of the garden. In the cleft of a rock nearby, where her master had told her to look, she found a box hewn from ice-clear crystal. When she opened it, a faint, bitter scent rose from the bright green paste inside. The boy wriggled and twisted in her arms, but at last she touched the ointment to his eyes. At once he was still,

staring past Cherry into the empty air. He took little notice of her for the rest of the day, and she busied herself in the garden while he played his solitary games.

Over the weeks Cherry got used to the work about the house and spent more and more time in the garden. The master was often there, waiting to reward his pretty servant with a kiss. Each day she bathed the boy and touched his eyes with unguent, then marveled at its dramatic effect. Gradually her curiosity increased.

One day she could overcome it no longer. The boy had wandered off after his bath. Cherry purposefully dawdled as she returned the crystal box to its hiding-place. When she was sure that she was alone, she dipped a finger into the ointment and rubbed it into her eyes. A scorching pain seared them and she staggered to the spring. After splashing her face again and again, she found that she could open her eyes without any pain. There, beneath the gentle bubbling of the spring's surface, she saw tiny people, men and women who could fit inside her

Touching a forbidden unguent to her
eyes, a young girl discovered a hidden
world of fairies beneath the surface
of a garden spring.

A lethal antidote to hostile spells

The causes of painful ills and wasting diseases were invisible; sufferers laid the blame on malevolent magic and sought the counsel of a friendly sorcerer. After diligent inquiry, it was on occasion divined that the patient's sufferings were affected by the machinations of a hostile witch, acting either from simple malice or in revenge for a slight.

As the cause was magical, so was the cure. The sorcerer filled a glazed stone drinking jar—a jug with a painted face, round belly and narrow neck was reckoned as the ideal receptacle—with a mixture of blood, hair, nail parings and urine from the patient. Sometimes the practitioner would add pins, knotted threads and the heart of a small animal. This foul concoction was brought slowly to a boil over the kitchen fire at dead of night, with the sorcerer chanting the Lord's Prayer backward, at first slowly, then faster as the liquid began to bubble and emit vile fumes. As the bubbles rose in the brew, it was expected that the distant witch or warlock would be clutched by terrible cramps. If the sorcerer did not relent, the enemy was sure to die.

thimble. Cherry bent close to the water and watched as the sprites danced and spun in its depths. Women clustered around one of the men, kissing and petting him. Cherry stared at the diminutive figure—and recognized her master.

She turned away, her eyes stinging now with tears of fury. She had been living with fairies, creatures of wicked mischief. The gentleman who had seemed so grand, whose kindness and kisses she had welcomed, was not a man at all, but a being as elusive as dew or moonlight.

She ran through the garden toward the house. All around her she could see fairies cavorting, frolicking in the grass, among the flowers and through the treetops. She slammed the kitchen door behind her and huddled beside the kitchen fire. Evening came and with it her master, once again in smiling human guise. When he bent to kiss her cheek, Cherry slapped him, crying that he should save his attentions for the fairy girls who so obviously enjoyed them.

The fairy gentleman saw at once what she had done and drew back from her, shaking his head sadly. He could not keep a serving-girl whose curiosity overwhelmed her obedience. Early the next morning he took her back to the crossroads where he had found her. He left her there, and Cherry made her way safely back to her family. Yet, like all mortals who had glimpsed the fairy kingdom, she lived ever after with a longing to see the creatures just once more.

The unguent Cherry had used enabled her to see into a realm usually invisible to mortals; but there were other potions that had the opposite effect. Sometimes these could blind the victims to certain aspects of the scenes before their eyes. More frighteningly, they could deepen the beholder's vision, enabling him to see the reality beneath surface appearances. In a rockbound castle high in the Carpathian Mountains, a pair of bold outlaws discovered just how fearsome the powers of such an unguent could be.

The poor and powerless folk of the Hungarian highlands had a champion in the bandit Dobosz. He led a company of men who were not afraid to defy the oppressive Magyar lords. He lived in a mountain redoubt with his men, and it was there one night that he heard a knocking on the door. He opened it on a sleek-haired man dressed all in black, who announced himself as an envoy of the greatest lord of the region. The Voyevode wished, after many years of hostility and bloodshed, to make peace with Dobosz. He was holding a splendid ball in his castle that night and hoped the outlaw would be his honored guest.

Any normal man would have feared a trap and declined the invitation, but Dobosz disdained caution. He agreed to go in the company of his trusted friend Iwanczuk. Donning the plumed hats that were their only finery, the two men climbed into the waiting coach with the envoy and drove off.

Some hours later they reached the castle, perched high on a craggy peak. A military band sounded horns and drums as Dobosz mounted the steps. Many doors

Opening windows on a hidden world

Tantalizing in its proximity, the kingdom of the fairy races hovered somewhere just beyond human view. Its denizens cavorted in the forest glades and among the wild flowers of the meadows as mortal men and women walked past unseeing. But there were folk who knew how to penetrate the mysteries of this other realm. They sharpened their sight in secret by anointing their eyes with certain fragrant herbs infused in oil.

Ordinary oil was rendered enchanted by washing it with specially prepared rose and marigold water until it lost its golden hue and turned white. The mixture was then placed in a vial with buds of hollyhock, marigold, thyme and hazel, and grass gathered from a hillock known to be the haunt of fairies. Set to strengthen for three days in the sun, the unguent could then be used to open the eyes of the mortal seeker.

swung open and he strode into a ballroom lighted by a thousand candles. A swarm of lackeys, very like the Voyevode's emissary in their black frock coats, crowded around the bandits, smiling and bowing.

Dobosz brushed them away and joined the guests. Although richly clad in silks and jewels, they seemed to him a sickly collection. Pale and slight, stiffly posed beside their ladies, not one of the men stood taller than the bandit's shoulder. They answered politely, even humbly, when he spoke to them, but no laughter or conversation filled the air.

Dobosz was despairing of any enjoyment when the envoy darted up to him. Behind him came the imposing figure of the Voyevode. As he bowed to the outlaw, the guests and lackeys alike drew around in silence. Iwanczuk felt as though a performance were about to begin and, indeed, when the nobleman spoke, the words hardly seemed to be his own. Glancing nervously at his envoy, he said that he hoped Dobosz would feel at home in the castle. As the bandit nodded at this pleasantry, the Voyevode added, "Not just for tonight, but for all time." He offered Dobosz a ring of golden keys.

Dobosz and Iwanczuk stared at each other in bewilderment. Seeing their surprise, the Voyevode explained that he had no heirs and that Dobosz was famed as an honorable man. He had only to accept the keys and the castle would be his.

Dobosz looked around the ballroom with its tall windows arching toward a frescoed ceiling, its polished floor reflecting sparkling chandeliers. This could never be the stronghold of a warrior nor the home of a simple man. He turned again to the Voyevode. The honor was too great for him, he answered. If the Voyevode wished to give up his castle, let it be made into a church for all the people, sanctified to the glory of God.

As Dobosz's last word rang through the room, the whole company of nobles, servants and musicians seemed to sag. The Voyevode swayed and fell to the floor. The lackeys dropped to their hands and knees, tongues lolling from their mouths. Dobosz bent to help his host, but Iwanczuk kept his eyes on the servants. They were crawling or dragging themselves down the room toward a burnished font, from which they scooped out dollops of an oily salve they then touched to their eyes. At once, they rose back to their feet and resumed their duties. The envoy anointed the eyes of his stricken lord, who sat up with new strength.

Soon everything was as it had been before. Amid the confusion Iwanczuk sidled off unnoticed toward the font and dipped one finger in the unguent. He touched the potion to his right eyelid, and at once he felt the room dissolve around him. A dizzying sea of shapes, colors and sounds washed over him until he clapped a hand to his other eye. At that all fell still. The only sound was the shriek of the night wind. Iwanczuk found himself standing amid the rubble of a ruined castle lighted by the moon. The bare skeletons of trees growing up through holes in the shattered floors swayed in the wind. Slinking about the fallen masonry was a pack of

When the bold bandit Dobosz was invited to a ball, he was startled by the offer of the keys of the castle in which it was held.

An ointment opened the eyes of Dobosz's
henchman, revealing their companions
to be bare trees and snarling hounds.

sleek black dogs with lolling tongues. When the bandit looked out over one broken wall and saw that the ruin was spinning above the cliffs, he staggered back in terrified understanding.

This was the devil's castle, known by all God-fearing men to whirl near the summit of the mountain called Pietros. The guests at the splendid ball were the blasted trees swaying in the unearthly wind and the lackeys were the hounds of hell. Trembling, Iwanczuk blinked, then opened his left eye. Once again, the ballroom glittered with candlelight.

Iwanczuk rushed to his friend's side. The Voyevode was urging Dobosz to reconsider. Iwanczuk realized that Dobosz

Fleeing the trap that had been set for them, the two brigands turned
to find the castle spinning like a top on the mountain's summit.

would commit his soul to the inferno if he accepted the keys that the Prince of Darkness himself was offering. He whispered to Dobosz that they were in the midst of great evil and must escape. Although the chieftain could see no danger among these pallid aristocrats, he took his comrade at his word. They edged their way toward the door. The lackeys, black hair bristling and smiles twisting into snarls, closed around them.

"God keep you all!" Iwanczuk shouted to them. At the sound of the holy name the lackeys fell back, crawling once again toward the font.

The outlaws ran out into the night, leaping across boulders to the safety of the forest. Gasping for breath, Iwanczuk told Dobosz the truth about the castle. The bandit chieftain shook his head in wonder, almost in disbelief, for he had seen neither devils nor dogs.

Iwanczuk bathed his right eye in the first clear mountain pool they found and in every stream they crossed on the long journey home. Yet the unguent that bestowed both the power to sustain illusion and the power to see through it would not wash away.

Ever afterward, he had only to close one eye to glimpse the devil slipping through a crowd or lurking in a corner. Born cautious, Iwanczuk grew ever more so, threading a careful path through infernal mischief that only he could see.

Chapter Five

Lapidary Lore

Delved from the earth's secret places or brought into being by the wiles of demons, gods and sorcerers: Such were the origins of the stones, jewels and precious gems that lent their energies to enchantment.

To catch and tame the energies entrapped even in a humble earth-stone took skill and knowledge. The dark, gleaming lodestone, for example, was known to all for its eerie attraction for iron, and those versed in the rudiments of magic lore could use its uncanny tugging to bring together lovers pulled apart by misfortune. Others, more advanced in study, appreciated the living soul the stone contained, and told how its emanations snatched the shoes from horses, drew nails and even levitated statues. But the wisest magicians went further, and they kept their secrets to themselves.

In adept hands and with the proper incantations, a lodestone could cure insanity or raise the phantoms of the dead, set fire to water or ease the pangs of childbirth. And there were ways to revive its powers, should they ever flag. Sometimes it was enough to bathe the

Harder than iron, stronger than stone, the jewel called Shamir was hidden from humankind,
and only the moorhen knew its whereabouts. But King Solomon, master of magic, encased
the bird's nestlings in glass until she brought forth the Shamir to set them free.

stone in precious linseed oil and bury it in the earth; but a lodestone was a living thing and had to be fed—with iron filings or, if all else failed, with blood.

Some useful talismans came not from the earth but from the things that crawl upon it. Inside the heads of certain reptiles, enfolded in their little brains, magicians occasionally discovered stones of startling potency. A tortoise might yield an enchanted pebble with the power to quench flames. Europe's witches hunted frogs and toads, whose skulls often bore miracle-working gems.

Others looked skyward for their occult treasure. A venturesome sorcerer could hope to find inside an eagle's nest a scarlet stone that promised its owner wealth and protection from evil chance. Backed by the right technique, the stone would also detect a guilty thief—but its loss was a grievous blow to the eagles, which could not breed without its help.

Birds played a vital part in the quest for the most remarkable stone of all—the fabulous Shamir. According to the elder legends of the Hebrews, the Shamir had been one of the miracles of Creation, a barleycorn-sized object that could smash iron and slice through rock like butter. It had been used by Moses, so some said, to carve sacred inscriptions in places where the Law forbade the use of metal; but all agreed that it had been lost utterly on the death of the great patriarch.

That misfortune seemed most acute in the days when Solomon was building the temple, the glory of his reign. Priests reminded the King that the temple's great stone blocks could not lawfully be hewn by anything so base as iron. They spoke of the Shamir, but added that it had vanished, centuries before, and now lay beyond the reach of mortal men. Yet Solomon could achieve what common mortals could not, for he was not only King of Israel and acknowledged as the wisest man of his age; he was also famed as a master magician. Marshaling his energies, he summoned up the Prince of demons, Ashmodai himself, to tell the secret. It was not easy even for Solomon to bind Ashmodai to his will; but at last the deed was done.

"What do you want with me, mighty King?" the demon snarled.

"With you, nothing," retorted Solomon. "But for my temple I must have the Shamir."

"Then ask the moorhen," sneered Ashmodai. "She uses it to split the barren mountainside to make crevices where green trees and plants may grow."

The King took the demon at his word, and sent his servants to find the moorhen's nest. When they tracked it down, they saw that it was full of chicks. The King used some of his fabled wisdom: He had the nest covered with a dome of glass. When the moorhen returned, she was frantic; she could see her young without being able to reach them. Then she flew off, and came back with the Shamir in her beak. At its touch, the glass shattered. A servant seized the Shamir, and Solomon had his wish.

With the Shamir, the rose-gold limestone that had been selected for the temple was effortlessly cut into perfect blocks, free of contamination by the masons' workaday iron tools. The shaping of the temple masonry was only one of the tasks that it performed for Solomon. The Shamir also had a role in the carving of Solomon's seal, most potent of all the gems of power This seal, in the form of an enchanted signet ring, guaranteed Solomon's authority over demons, jinn and other spirits, and allowed him to converse with birds and the beasts. Without it, he was no mightier than any other mortal, at least according to one account.

The King, so that story goes, had become arrogant in his power; to punish him, God had the ring snatched from him and thrown into the sea. For three years, Solomon wandered as a beggar in his own kingdom, while a mocking demon assumed his likeness and his throne. Only when God relented, and the ring turned up in the belly of a fish, did the humiliated monarch return to his former glory. But soon, with the passing of Solomon's age of grandeur and of wisdom, the Shamir disappeared again.

It was never forgotten, yet in later, less blessed years, no one could remember just exactly what it was. A diamond, said those who knew that jewel's purity and hardness; mere emery, said others, who had traced its name through every alphabet and language, back through the incunabula and grimoires to the dusty, faded vellum and the crumbling papyrus of a vanished world. Some sages, deeply versed in all the fragments that remained of its rich lore, declared that the Shamir was not a stone or a jewel but a worm: a worm both miniature and miraculous, whose small, adamantine jaws pierced crystal, rock or steel at its master's will.

As for the ring itself, it was variously believed to be forged from bands of silver and copper, or made of heavy iron. The marks of power that were engraved upon it were said to include pentacles and words of binding from the ancient Phoenician tongue; or the design upon the seal was of stars nestling within stars, and the words around the ring were Hebrew. Given such an array of descriptions, reconstruction was an impossible task, although a thousand generations of magicians were not deterred from trying.

Even if the fabulous power of Solomon and his seal had vanished forever from the world of men, much could still be achieved by means of "ordinary" precious and semiprecious stones; and the lapidaries who cut and sold such gems often compiled meticulous lists of their properties. Many stones had strong associations with the planets and the zodiac, and were best used or worn under the guidance of a skilled astrologer. But even without their celestial correspondences, certain gemstones had no small influence on the health and wealth of their owners.

Queen of them all was the diamond, brilliant and all-healing, especially in cases of mental illness. A symbol of divinity, it protected its wearer against plague and unseen ill-wishers, turning dark to warn of the presence of poison in an innocent-looking dish of food. To the faint-hearted, it brought relief from the terrors of the night, and to the brave it promised strength and victory.

The ruby, like the diamond, would guard against pestilence and poison, and, though it could not match the curative power of the diamond, it had one very useful property of its own: When danger loomed, a ruby would change its color to alert its owner.

Other gemstones also changed their color, often for very specific reasons. The opal generally brought good luck, and in some cases could inspire its wearer to foretell the future. But a loss of its precious luster was a sure sign of failing health. The variety of garnet known as the carbuncle was especially prized in time of plague. If an infected victim should draw near to the owner of the carbuncle, the deep-red gem would fade, as a warning of danger.

Sapphire and lapis lazuli—even the most ancient of authorities sometimes confused the two—never lost their perfect blue, but were relied upon as painkillers. Water in which either gemstone had been dipped was a certain

Forbidden by priests to use base metal for cutting the stones of the temple,
Solomon employed the Shamir to hew building blocks and carve inscriptions.

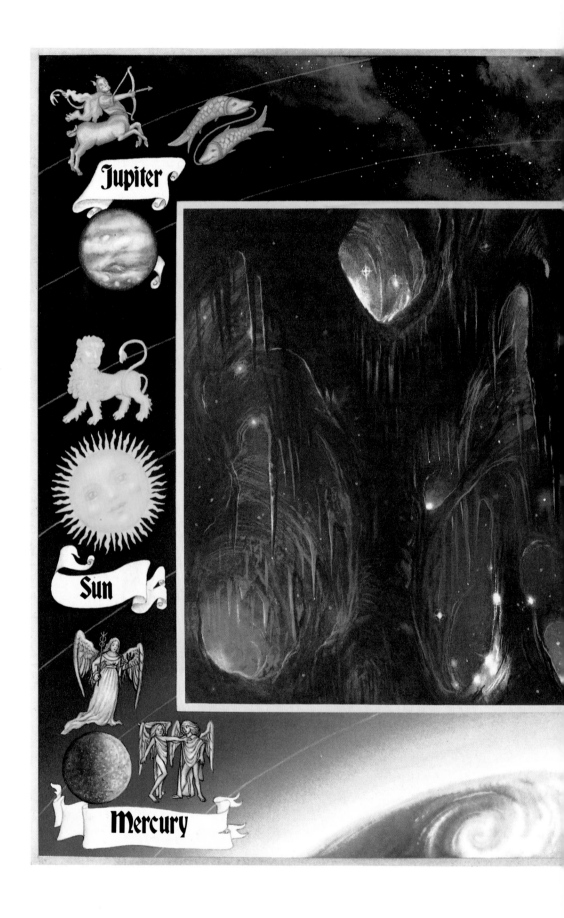

Jupiter

Sun

Mercury

The chain of cosmic connections

Between the heavenly bodies and the human world stretched a web of correspondence and affinities that was diligently explored by students of arcane lore. The sun, the moon and the five known planets were all linked to specific zodiacal signs. In addition, each of them was held to govern a skill and a day of the week, as well as a particular color, stone and precious metal.

Sunday was ruled by the sun, whose gleaming light was reflected in its talismans—gold, diamond and topaz. It was a good day for acquiring wealth and winning powerful friends. The pale moon controlled Monday and the destinies of travelers at sea, who, by wearing white garments and ornaments of silver and pearl, might guarantee a safe voyage. Mars, with its ruddy glow, sent soldiers into battle on Tuesday, carrying the standards of the wargod: iron and bloodred rubies. Fleet-footed Mercury, the messenger of the gods, fostered commerce. Wednesday's patron, he favored quicksilver, the muted tones of gray, and shimmering opals.

On Thursdays, Jupiter, clothed in royal blue, presided over the health of mortals with his emblems, tin and amethyst. Pleasure-seeking Venus lent her graceful presence to Friday, providing luck in love to those who displayed her tokens— the green of growing things, emeralds and shining copper. Baleful Saturn lent special power to lead and onyx. The stability of the distant and unwavering planet ensured the success of building works begun on Saturday, but its dark side made injuries more likely.

Magicians used their knowledge of the astrological connections to enhance their spells. They could, for example, give added strength to a love potion by making it in a copper chalice on a green cloth on a Friday. Venus would then be sure to cast a favorable aspect over their work.

Branches of pink, calcareous coral, gathered from the sea bed, deflected demons, soothed sickness, warded off nightmares and averted the Evil Eye.

cure for eye troubles; a lapis bracelet would protect a child from illness, and a sapphire preserved chastity.

Emerald, too, could cure eye ailments. But when used as a defense against vipers, it had an opposite effect: It struck them blind. It shared the sapphire's chaste influence and generally promoted love and understanding. Emerald would also prevent epileptic fits.

The deep, dark green of jade granted it similar powers as an ocular remedy. And jade was thought to bring good luck. In eastern lands, merchants reckoned that a small piece of the stone clenched in the fist would guarantee the profitable outcome of a business deal.

Amethyst had the convenient power of preventing drunkenness. To benefit from its full effect, some insisted that the gem must be worn in the navel; others swore that its proper place was beneath the drinker's tongue. Bishops of the Church simply set amethyst in their rings—though less for its sobering effect than out of respect for its long tradition as the gem of the high priests.

Settings, in fact, could be almost as important as the stones themselves. Amethyst, for instance, worked best in a silver mounting, though, as a rule, a golden setting greatly increased the power of almost any stone. Judicious engraving, both of setting and of stone, was another way to multiply the effective potency of a charm. For example, a sea-green beryl, set in gold, was known to bring love and friendship, but such an outcome was only assured if the gem had been incised with the image of a frog. And the white crystals of chalcedony, which could grant protection to a traveler, must first be carved in the likeness of a galloping horseman with a pike in his right hand. Emerald's powers might be reinforced by the carving of a starling. Sapphire was improved by the etching of a ram.

The adroit use of images, letters and cryptic runes was as important a part of a lapidary's skills as the selection of the appropriate gem. Many a learned treatise was devoted to the choice of the correct words for an inscription. The names Jasper, Melchior and Balthazar, which tradition ascribed to the Magi who brought gifts to the infant Jesus, were known to possess a general curative effect. For a more precise action—to help out in a case of unrequited love, to guard against assault by witchcraft or simply to assuage a toothache—it might be necessary to search long and deep in the ancient texts of prophecy and magic.

The amulet might take the form of a brooch, a bracelet or a medallion. Rings, though, were generally favored. A ring was compact and difficult to steal, for it was almost part of the wearer's body, and according to need it could be ostentatious or discreet. Best of all, safely hidden on the ring's inner surface, a well-chosen charm could do its work in quiet secrecy.

No later rings, alas, could ever match the power and authority of Solomon's great lost seal. But it was known that some of them, at least, could cast a fair enchantment. Naturally they were never commonplace, and indeed they left their mark on the legends of the world.

So it was with the ring of the Princess Frastrada. She was a beautiful and accomplished young woman of noble birth, and in the ordinary course of things she would have needed no magical assistance to find a suitable husband. But she had set her sights high. Not only was she determined to be a Queen, but she would be Queen to Charlemagne himself, King of France and Holy Emperor of the western world. The chroniclers did not record how the magic ring came into her possession; it may have been a bequest from some ancestress who dabbled in the darker arts. But from her greenest youth she knew the golden circlet's capabilities and used them to further her ambitions.

In due course she had her way, and, given her high rank and exalted human charms, it was not so remarkable a thing. But Charlemagne was no longer in the first flush of youth; he had had three wives before her and, besides, he was careworn with the burdens of his Empire. In a little time, his courtiers predicted, he would tire of his new bride.

Instead, the aging Emperor's passion burned bright and constant as a star. Night or day, he knew no happiness when he was not beside his Queen. Neither he nor any of his courtiers suspected an enchantment, and for a time everything went well.

But Frastrada's ring could only guarantee her Charlemagne's devotion, as its shapers had intended. It gave her no other protection, and when, still in the springtime of her marriage, she sickened with a mortal illness, the ring was powerless to help. She had achieved her life's ambition and would have died content, but one thing pained her fading heart: the thought that another woman, after she was gone, might use her ring to steal the Emperor's affections. Unattended for a moment, she slid the ring from her finger and hid it in her mouth, so that it might be buried with her. Then she died.

Living liquid turned to stone

Ancient poets claimed that trees wept tears, which fell to the ground and hardened into amber. Others opined that amber was pure sunlight frozen into stone. Dimly translucent, its misty depths seemed to trap the light of long-vanished days. Even the remains of living things— forgotten plantlife and unknown insects—could sometimes be seen entombed within it. Small wonder that, through the ages, amber was credited with mystical powers.

Sometimes it was used as a medicine. Ground up and mixed with honey, it strengthened the eyes. If rose oil was added, it could sharpen the ears against deafness.

Other physicians preserved its beauty by enjoining its use as a talisman. Strung into necklaces or bracelets, drops of amber guarded their wearer from a host of ailments, from ague to the croup. The King of Persia wore a necklace said to be made of amber that fell from heaven in the time of the Prophet. So mighty were the ornament's powers that the ruler feared no danger while under its protection.

Charlemagne was almost mad with grief. Great funeral pomp was planned for the dead Queen, but the Emperor could not bear the thought of her lying in the darkness and solitude of the tomb. Distraught, he maintained a hopeless vigil in Frastrada's chambers, ignoring the pleas of his court and even that of Turpin, his friend and highest counselor.

At length Turpin suspected sorcery. He waited until Charlemagne fell into an exhausted sleep. Then he crept silently to the dead Queen's side. He searched her neck, hands and ears for the talisman he was certain must exist, but found nothing. Just as he was about to admit defeat, his torchlight glinted on gold. Turpin opened Frastrada's icy, half-parted lips and drew forth the ring.

The effect was as immediate as it was miraculous. Charlemagne awoke at once and saw his friend. "Turpin, most faithful of my counselors!" he cried. "You shall be by my side forever." Almost absent-mindedly, the Emperor gave orders for the burial to proceed. The crisis seemed over, and the busy imperial court heaved a great sigh of relief.

For Turpin, however, the crisis was only beginning. Charlemagne insisted that his counselor never leave his presence. He knew no peace. Worse still, the rest of the court grew increasingly jealous of the Emperor's blatant favoritism, and the atmosphere around the throne grew thick and tense. Turpin had

Of his four wives, none captivated Charlemagne so strongly as the lady Frastrada. When she died, a nobleman found the secret of her allure: a magic ring concealed on her person.

been the monarch's loyal friend for many years and had no need of the ring's assistance to keep his high position. But the charm's power appalled him; as Charlemagne's shrewdest adviser, he knew the damage that would be done if it fell into the hands of a less devoted servant. So he kept the secret to himself and shouldered the burden as best he could.

Gradually, the strain grew unendurable. It reached a peak one summer night, in the course of a royal progress from south to north across the Emperor's great domains. The party had encamped in a forest, and all but Turpin were sleeping soundly. Restless with worry and fatigue, he wandered awhile amid the moonlit trees. Each step he took from his master eased the pressure that he felt; and when at last he stood beside an exquisite pool in the forest, he experienced something like relief.

He took out the ring and looked at it, as he had done so many times before. The signs and symbols written on it meant nothing to him, though he knew their power. But this time, in the moonlight, he noticed the figure of a swan, which he had never seen before. Almost without thinking, he threw the ring outward, into the pool. And as it sank, a swan, ghostly in the moonlight, passed silently over the spot where it had fallen.

The next day, the Emperor greeted Turpin as the old friend he was, and not as the object of a dark obsession. But as the royal servants struck camp and prepared to move off, Charlemagne began to show a reluctance to leave. He bade them cease their packing. "We shall pass today hunting, here in the forest," he ordered.

Turpin was worried, and rightly. For it so befell that Charlemagne, leading the hunt, found himself before the pool that held Frastrada's ring. To the Emperor, this was the most beautiful place in the world. He drank deeply of the water and let his old eyes linger on the graceful swans whose home it was. Then he blew a great blast on his hunting horn to summon his scattered courtiers.

When they arrived, led by an alarmed Turpin, the Emperor declared, "Here would I stay forever. I have never seen such beauty." Only when evening fell could he be persuaded to leave the spot, much to his chief counselor's relief. And even then, the Emperor would not go until he had made a vow. "By this pool," he swore, "I shall build the greatest palace of my Empire. From this place shall I rule, and here shall I leave my bones."

And all that he had vowed came to pass. The palace was built, and in time there grew around it the great imperial capital of Aix-la-Chapelle. A fine cathedral was raised there, too; and in its vaults the Emperor lay, obedient even in death to the old enchantment of a master lapidary's magic ring.

The ring remained in its tranquil pool, although the spell faded with the turning of a thousand years and more. But it never faded altogether. Sometimes by moonlight it regained its power, wise men said. Those who passed close to its resting-place at such an hour would feel its tug forever after, and forever long to return.

To break the spell upon the monarch, the ring was cast into a lake. But Charlemagne, drawn by its power, resolved to build a palace on the shore and end his days there.

A Sage's Golden Quest

Of all the guardians of the hidden lore, none were more jealous of their secrets than the alchemists, specialists in transmuting base metals into gold. Only adepts knew the formula that controlled the transformation, and each master, according to tradition, was allowed to pass on his knowledge to just one disciple. The revelation did not in itself guarantee success; only a man who had driven egotism from his soul could have the purity of spirit necessary to refine ordinary matter into the world's most precious metal.

One who mastered the art was an Englishman named Thomas Charnock, who was born in the days when science and magic had not yet grown apart. He took up the quest as a young scholar, equipped only with a scanty store of Latin and a small inherited income. With its aid, he traveled the country in search of a master to initiate him.

After some months he heard talk of a prior in the city of Bath reputed to have alchemical powers. He tracked the man down, only to find that his knowledge had not brought him happiness. Overmuch study had left him blind, and the small boy he paid to lead him informed Charnock that the old man's wits were going too. Nonetheless, he possessed the formula, and from his disconnected ramblings, the younger man learned all that he needed to know.

The details of the formula he received were lost when the line of alchemical knowledge came to an end. Chroniclers suggested, though, that the process involved subjecting a weak solution of gold to a complex cycle of twelve separate distillations. If the seeker was on the right track, he could expect first to create a hard, white pebble. Later, the white would turn to red. The resulting russet nugget was known to alchemists as the philosopher's stone. A mystical substance, it could not merely turn ordinary metals into gold, but improved everything in its kind: Thus, if used on humans, it was also a sure cure for disease and an elixir of youth.

Burning with enthusiasm to put his newly acquired knowledge to the test, Charnock used his small funds to equip a laboratory in his gloomy country mansion. He sought out the finest equipment from metal-workers and glassblowers; to conceal the true nature of his work, he spun wild tales of a plan to make a brazen head that would speak and keep him company in the long winter nights. He preserved his privacy from the prying eyes of neighbors by draping the windows of his study with thick curtains rarely opened to let in light.

At last all the utensils were in place, the retorts gleaming and the fire lighted. Jars of gold pieces, silver, mercury, ammonia and aqua fortis lined the wooden shelves, vying for space with leather-bound books and dusty parchments inscribed in crabbed and ancient hands. Guided by the lessons contained in these manuscripts as well as by the prior's directions, Charnock dropped flakes of gold into a flask of acid to start the long process of manufacture.

After each cycle of evaporation and condensation, the substance in

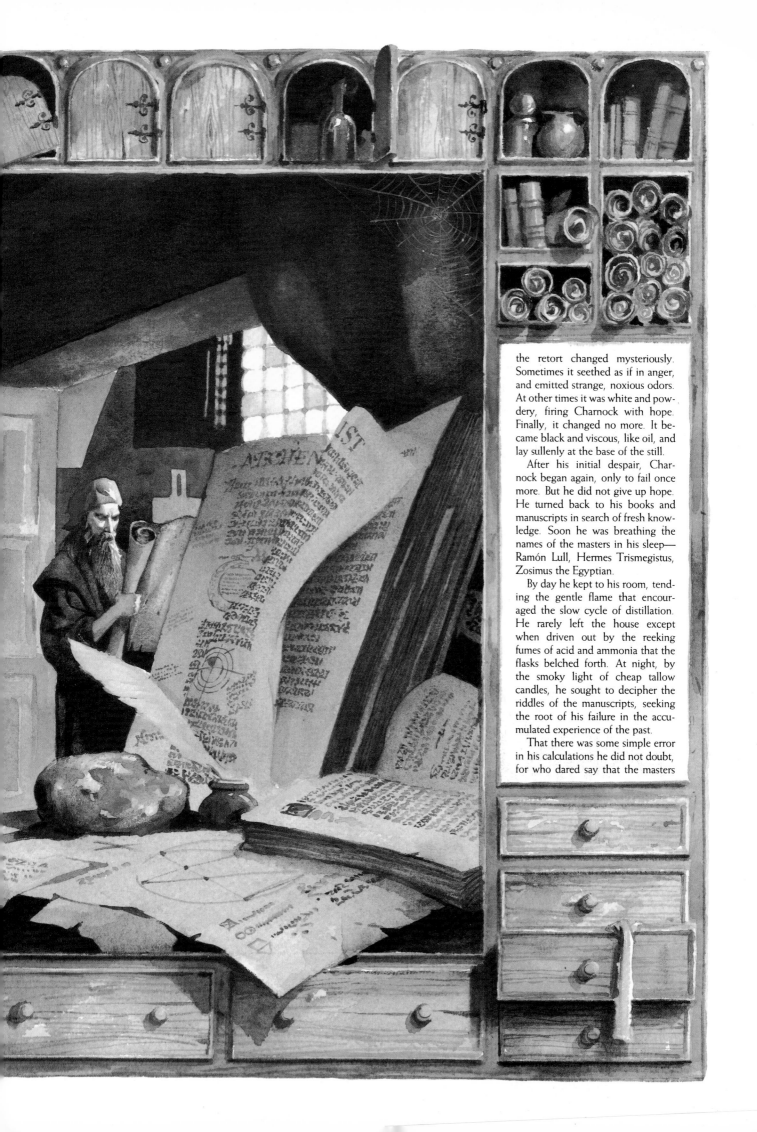

the retort changed mysteriously. Sometimes it seethed as if in anger, and emitted strange, noxious odors. At other times it was white and powdery, firing Charnock with hope. Finally, it changed no more. It became black and viscous, like oil, and lay sullenly at the base of the still.

After his initial despair, Charnock began again, only to fail once more. But he did not give up hope. He turned back to his books and manuscripts in search of fresh knowledge. Soon he was breathing the names of the masters in his sleep—Ramón Lull, Hermes Trismegistus, Zosimus the Egyptian.

By day he kept to his room, tending the gentle flame that encouraged the slow cycle of distillation. He rarely left the house except when driven out by the reeking fumes of acid and ammonia that the flasks belched forth. At night, by the smoky light of cheap tallow candles, he sought to decipher the riddles of the manuscripts, seeking the root of his failure in the accumulated experience of the past.

That there was some simple error in his calculations he did not doubt, for who dared say that the masters

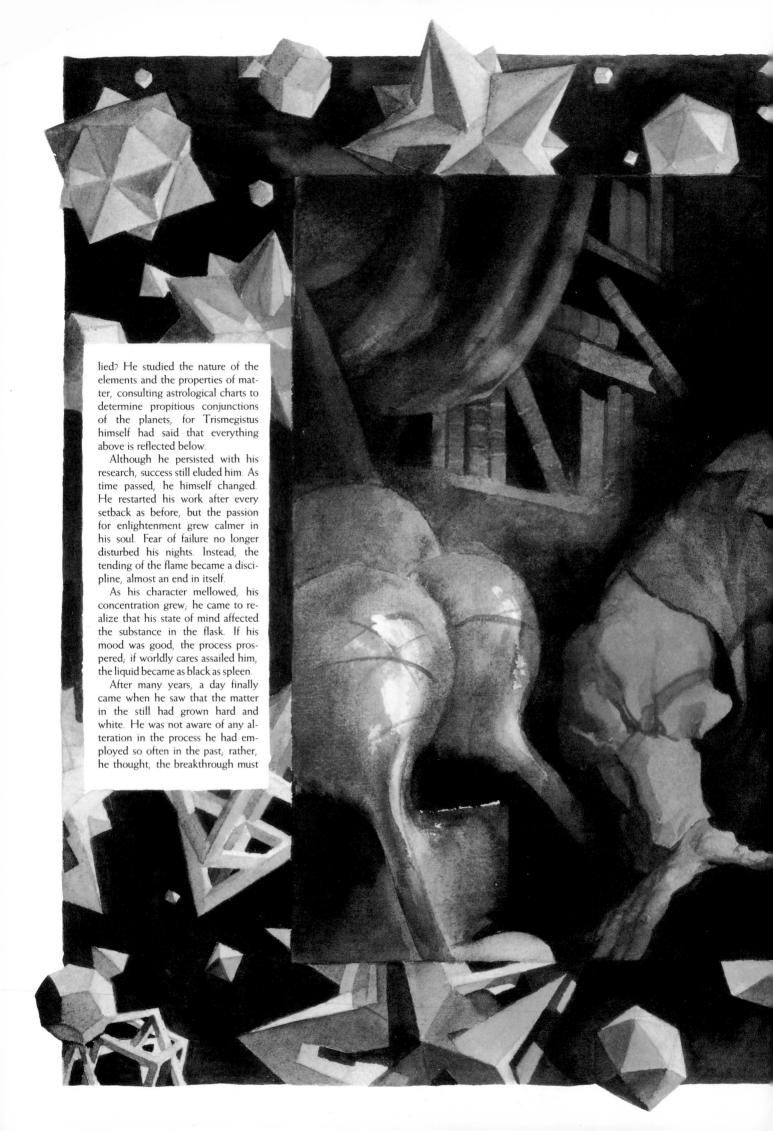

lied? He studied the nature of the elements and the properties of matter, consulting astrological charts to determine propitious conjunctions of the planets, for Trismegistus himself had said that everything above is reflected below.

Although he persisted with his research, success still eluded him. As time passed, he himself changed. He restarted his work after every setback as before, but the passion for enlightenment grew calmer in his soul. Fear of failure no longer disturbed his nights. Instead, the tending of the flame became a discipline, almost an end in itself.

As his character mellowed, his concentration grew; he came to realize that his state of mind affected the substance in the flask. If his mood was good, the process prospered; if worldly cares assailed him, the liquid became as black as spleen.

After many years, a day finally came when he saw that the matter in the still had grown hard and white. He was not aware of any alteration in the process he had employed so often in the past; rather, he thought, the breakthrough must

reflect the change in himself. Calmly, betraying no agitation, he continued the cycle of distillation. Charnock watched in awe as a red flush spread across the white, until the stone had turned the color of blood. With a mounting sense of triumph, he lifted it from the retort, chipped off a flake and dropped it into a caldron of molten lead. The bubbling metal fizzed and hardened, and as it did so it was suffused with a rich yellow glow. After twenty years of effort, Thomas Charnock had finally reached his goal.

As a young man he might have used his skill to make himself rich, but the quest had taken away his taste for worldly show. Instead he lived quietly and comfortably for the few years of life that remained to him, and his neighbors noted in him an aura of saintly calm. The lesson he had learned in the course of his long pursuit was an old one, that it is the journey, not the arrival, that matters. He had come to see that the change his mission had wrought in himself was more important than any of the transmutations achieved in all his bubbling retorts.

Chapter Six

Mirrors and Metals

Mirrors opened windows into other worlds, perfect replicas of our own but always alien. Sages in many lands recognized and sought to harness the arcane powers residing in the silvered glass. Mirrors from the time of the Three Kingdoms, damascened with precious metal and bristling with amethysts and turquoises, defended the ancient Chinese from the menaces of demons: Confronted by its own likeness, an evil spirit would howl in anguish and stumble away to die. Legend has it that, at Syracuse, Archimedes, master of machinery, concentrated the blistering heat of the Ionian sun in a burning-mirror—and thus consumed a Roman fleet with flame. Shielding their eyes from the blaze, the Greek elders reminded their amazed young warriors that it was with mirrors, not flints, that the god Prometheus created fire.

In the Dark Ages, when leprosy and plague first crawled into the villages of Europe, families learned to turn a mirror's face to the wall if someone in the household died—and quickly. The mirror was a window from the world of the envious

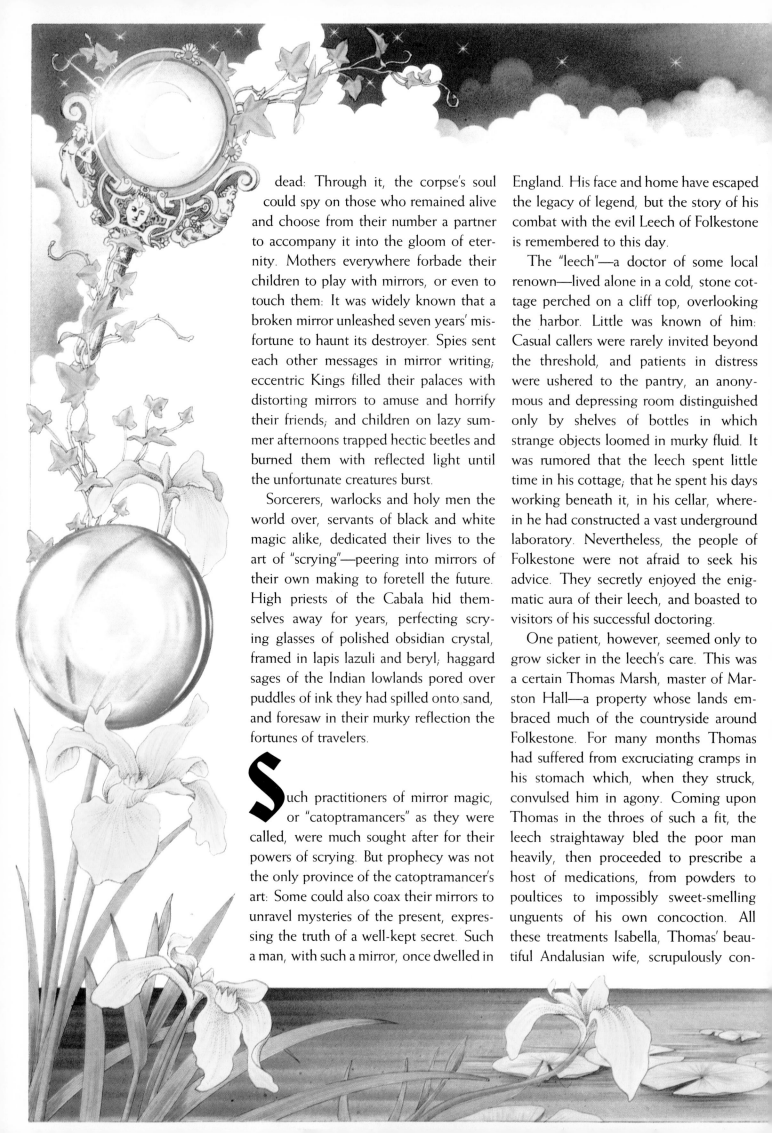

dead: Through it, the corpse's soul could spy on those who remained alive and choose from their number a partner to accompany it into the gloom of eternity. Mothers everywhere forbade their children to play with mirrors, or even to touch them: It was widely known that a broken mirror unleashed seven years' misfortune to haunt its destroyer. Spies sent each other messages in mirror writing; eccentric Kings filled their palaces with distorting mirrors to amuse and horrify their friends; and children on lazy summer afternoons trapped hectic beetles and burned them with reflected light until the unfortunate creatures burst.

Sorcerers, warlocks and holy men the world over, servants of black and white magic alike, dedicated their lives to the art of "scrying"—peering into mirrors of their own making to foretell the future. High priests of the Cabala hid themselves away for years, perfecting scrying glasses of polished obsidian crystal, framed in lapis lazuli and beryl; haggard sages of the Indian lowlands pored over puddles of ink they had spilled onto sand, and foresaw in their murky reflection the fortunes of travelers.

Such practitioners of mirror magic, or "catoptramancers" as they were called, were much sought after for their powers of scrying. But prophecy was not the only province of the catoptramancer's art: Some could also coax their mirrors to unravel mysteries of the present, expressing the truth of a well-kept secret. Such a man, with such a mirror, once dwelled in England. His face and home have escaped the legacy of legend, but the story of his combat with the evil Leech of Folkestone is remembered to this day.

The "leech"—a doctor of some local renown—lived alone in a cold, stone cottage perched on a cliff top, overlooking the harbor. Little was known of him: Casual callers were rarely invited beyond the threshold, and patients in distress were ushered to the pantry, an anonymous and depressing room distinguished only by shelves of bottles in which strange objects loomed in murky fluid. It was rumored that the leech spent little time in his cottage; that he spent his days working beneath it, in his cellar, wherein he had constructed a vast underground laboratory. Nevertheless, the people of Folkestone were not afraid to seek his advice. They secretly enjoyed the enigmatic aura of their leech, and boasted to visitors of his successful doctoring.

One patient, however, seemed only to grow sicker in the leech's care. This was a certain Thomas Marsh, master of Marston Hall—a property whose lands embraced much of the countryside around Folkestone. For many months Thomas had suffered from excruciating cramps in his stomach which, when they struck, convulsed him in agony. Coming upon Thomas in the throes of such a fit, the leech straightaway bled the poor man heavily, then proceeded to prescribe a host of medications, from powders to poultices to impossibly sweet-smelling unguents of his own concoction. All these treatments Isabella, Thomas' beautiful Andalusian wife, scrupulously continued to administer in the following months, but her husband's condition only deteriorated further.

Throughout Thomas' long ordeal, the leech called at Marston Hall regularly, professing himself baffled and intrigued by the malady. Thomas, despite his continued sufferings, found the doctor's interest reassuring: He trusted his analytical perspicacity and judgment.

And so he was easily persuaded to comply when one day the leech determined upon a radical assault on the disease. Having subjected his patient's belly to the fury of wasps caged in an upended bell jar, the doctor suddenly pulled Thomas upright and pronounced him cured. Pleased though he was to hear the news, Thomas was obliged to observe that he was nevertheless yet in great pain. Favoring him with a rare smile, the leech assured him that the cramps that still assailed him were merely the dregs of his long anguish. He should go for a ride: The wind would soon blow them away. With these words, the doctor turned on his heel and left.

His heart pounding with excitement, Thomas limped over to the window and shouted down to his stableboy, Ralph, to saddle the horses: That very day they would ride together to nearby Ostenhanger and see the goose fair. The groom complied. Thomas mounted his roan with great difficulty and, his gaunt face creased with pain, trotted off into the fields, with Ralph riding behind. His wife ran after him a little way: In a mixture of Spanish and disjointed English, she implored him not to go. Then she stopped and stood still. She seemed to be waiting for something. Her six-year-old daughter Marian watched the scene from the nearby orchard, where she had been playing unobserved.

Seeing her mother standing so pensively, she was about to run to her when she noticed the leech approaching from the gateway. The little girl hid behind a hedge and stared uncomprehendingly as the physician took the woman in his arms. He kissed her for a long time, then the two of them turned and went into the house. Confused and curious, Marian followed them. They went straight to her mother's bedroom. Squinting through a crack in the door, Marian could see them huddled around a small object on a table, handling it. Her mother laughed and kissed the leech again. Then they undressed and lay down on the bed.

Gray afternoon slid into night, and the pair at last fell asleep. As stealthy as a hunting cat, Marian crept into the room, took the object from the table and fled back to the sanctuary of the orchard. Only then did she dare look at her prize. It was a little doll, the figure of a man, lovingly fashioned: And in its stomach were embedded a mass of metal skewers. Wrinkling her nose in distaste, the little girl worked the barbs out of the body of her new-found toy.

Even as she labored, Thomas lay by the roadside, many miles from home. His screams, flung out to the nearby trees, were heard only by Ralph, who tightly gripped his master's hand as he squirmed

and twisted in the dirt. But suddenly, Thomas ceased to howl. Soaked in sweat, he sat up unsteadily and pronounced his fit finished. After a while, the two men continued gently on to Ostenhanger.

By the time they arrived, the fair was in full cry: Fire-eaters, freaks and fakirs from the Orient and Araby held the crowds spellbound. Thomas, a tall man, looked around over the heads of the throng until his gaze was arrested by an elderly man in sorcerer's robes, leaning on a staff before the entrance to a pavilion. The wizard was staring at him intently. Drawn by a force stronger than curiosity, Thomas found himself pushing through the crowd toward the magus, who beckoned him into the billowing tent.

Inside, Thomas found a massive iron bath, shaped disturbingly like a coffin. Dirty-looking liquid filled it almost to the top. Silently the old man indicated that Thomas should undress and get into the bath. To his own astonishment, Thomas meekly did as he was bidden.

The instant that he lay down, the rude shock of freezing water catapulted Thomas to his senses. Sitting bolt upright with a startled cry, he rapidly took

With the aid of a bath and a mirror, a fairground magician undertook to cure a stranger racked by a mysterious ailment.

stock of his weird surroundings. All about him were draped rich silks and thick tapestries. Skeletons of unfamiliar beasts hung suspended in space; the air was close and fogged with smoldering incense; and all was dominated by a huge mirror, in which Thomas could see himself reflected, pale and ludicrous in the candlelight. The old man grinned, seemingly amused by the situation.

Shaking with cold and seething with anger, Thomas demanded to know into what mischief he had been tricked. Had he fallen into the hands of a necromancer or some other practitioner of the black arts?

With a flowing movement surprising in its elegance, the old man swept off his sorcerer's skullcap and bowed low before Thomas. He introduced himself as Aldrovando, an Englishman despite his name; and catoptramancy was his science, not meddling in the affairs of the dead. He apologized for the simple subterfuge of hypnotizing Thomas, but time was very short—too short to explain the ritual necessities that had led to his patient's present situation.

By no means set at ease by this strange explanation, Thomas grasped the sides of the bath nervously. Time was short for what? But Aldrovando made no answer. His attention was fixed firmly on the mirror. The sorcerer began to murmur to himself, waving his head from side to side and passing his fingers across the glass. Then, to Thomas' amazement, the mirror began to hum like a spinning top. Before his eyes a picture began to resolve on its mottled surface. Thomas drew in his breath in horror. He could clearly see his own daughter, hunched in the corner of a darkened room. Her face bore the weals of a severe beating, and she was sobbing freely, her hands held up to her mouth in abject terror.

Aldrovando bent his head abruptly. His incantations grew louder. The picture in the mirror waned, then shone again more brilliantly than before, this time revealing Isabella and the leech poised before a tattered figurine. At once the old man turned. There was no humor in his glance. He spoke urgently, commanding Thomas to submerge himself entirely as soon as he gave the word. Thomas nodded dumbly, unable to tear his eyes away from the bizarre spectacle in the glass. The leech was now inspecting the edge of a rapier, and leveling its point at the breast of the figurine.

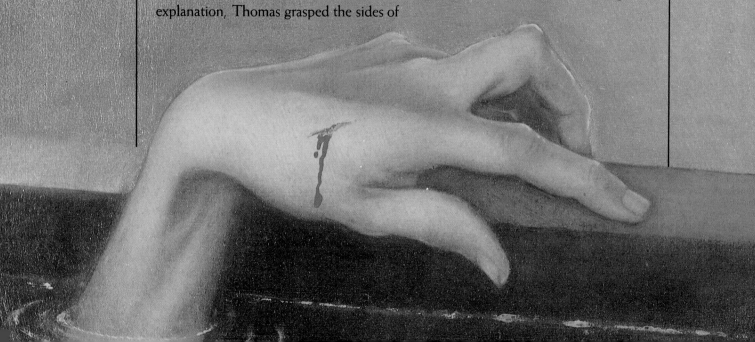

Suddenly Aldrovando cried out in an urgent voice: "Now! Under!"

Gulping down his breath, Thomas quickly slid beneath the surface of the liquid. A stench of rotting matter flooded his nose, and almost immediately he erupted into the air once again, choking and cursing like a tavern drunk. Aldrovando was standing very close to the mirror, studying it with intense concentration. Thomas cleared his eyes and leaned forward to see. The leech was gesticulating at Isabella, brandishing the hilt of his rapier at her. The sword's blade lay shattered at their feet.

Aldrovando growled with satisfaction, then shouted again in warning as the leech suddenly drew a skewer from his pocket and made to jab at the doll. Once more Thomas ducked, but not fast enough. As the leech's stabs first struck, Thomas' hands were not yet under the filthy surface of the liquid. Roaring in pain, he sat up at once to find the top of his left hand slashed open, as by a razor.

Aldrovando was again absorbed in scrutinizing the mirror. The leech had disappeared from view. Thomas could see Isabella weeping: She clutched her face where she, too, had been struck.

Then the leech moved back into the picture, dragging behind him Thomas' old harquebus. This monstrous gun, a relic of a foreign campaign long past, the leech hastily mounted on its support, aiming it squarely at the doll's head. Aldrovando turned and whipped down his hand. Filling his lungs with fetid air, Thomas plunged into the slimy fluid once again and remained there until he could bear it no longer. When he surfaced, he found himself quite alone. The picture in the mirror was fading, but Thomas could yet discern the body of the leech sprawled across the floor—his face exploded to a pulp of bloody meat.

It was some time before Ralph, who had become anxious for his master's safety, discovered Thomas. He found him still in the tent, balanced on the rim of a cast-iron coffin, naked, covered in foul-smelling filth, and gazing benignly at his own reflection in an ancient mirror.

From that night on, Thomas Marsh enjoyed improbably good health until the day he died. Of Isabella nothing was ever heard again. Some said that she fled back to Andalusia; others that her husband took radical steps to cure her of her infidelity. The leech was reportedly sighted at several places in England—despite the fact that his corpse had been publicly burned at Marston. Aldrovando, however, continued to ply his white magic for many years after saving the soul and body of Thomas Marsh, appearing in various guises to folk held prisoner by the forces of evil, and setting them free with the mystical power of mirrors.

Many such workers of wonders were itinerant, traveling to where their services were in demand and where new scope for their talents lay. Perhaps, too, they were driven ever onward by some inner demon that would not allow them to rest and put down roots like the good, ordinary folk whose ways they scorned but whose needs they served.

Trapped in the enchanter's web

The old lore had many stories of mirrors that were windows into different worlds. But out of Arthur's Britain came a tale of one that served instead as a barrier, set between an ill-starred maiden and the real world she was forbidden to gaze upon.

Chroniclers do not record who put the curse on the Lady of Shalott, nor why; and even she herself could not tell what punishment threatened if she fell afoul of her maledictor's bane. She knew only that she was condemned to live cloistered forever in a gray-walled island castle upstream from Camelot; she could not leave her room, nor even glance from its gabled window on the river and fields below.

Her only link with the outside world was the great mirror that hung upon the wall opposite the open casement. Before it stood a loom. She spent her days weaving an endless tapestry, capturing in fabric the shadow-images she received at second hand from the glass.

In the slow rhythms of her sheltered days the Lady had almost found contentment, when one morning a vision appeared in the mirror that rudely broke the spell. It was the boldest of Arthur's knights, Sir Lancelot, riding to his liege lord's court. She glimpsed his noble steed, the sun glinting from the knight's breastplate, the dark curls cascading from his plumed helm. It was the finest sight she had ever seen.

Forgetting the curse that hung over her, she stepped to the window. Impulsively, she looked out into the sunlight. At once the mirror shattered and the tapestry ripped asunder. With a despairing cry, she leaped back, but too late. She had brought down doom upon herself.

Her refuge gone, she left the tower and wandered, spellbound, down to the river. Later that day, courtiers noticed a small boat floating rudderless under the balconies of Camelot. In it lay the white-robed body of the Lady, who had forsaken the pale world of mirror images for the cold embrace of death.

A Romany ritual
to catch a thief

Among the Gypsies, who were as skilled in metalworking as they were wise in magic, the blacksmith's anvil was used as a ritual tool to detect thieves. The victim of a robbery would turn an anvil into an altar by hallowing it with a lighted candle, a pile of salt and a piece of bread. Around the anvil he would set utensils taken from every person who could have committed the crime. Then he would summon the suspects, and urge the guilty one to confess.

If no one came forward, he would ask each individual in turn to kiss the anvil and to strike it with a tool. Then all would join together in an oath calling down retribution. Driven by fears of an unspeakable, supernatural vengeance, the wrongdoer was compelled—even against his will—to return the spoil and beg forgiveness.

One group who roamed the lands in days past had learned to harness not only the magic of mirrors, but also of metal. These were the Gypsies—wanderers of the open road in every country of the European continent. Men and women feared the Gypsies, calling them the descendants of Cain, barred for eternity from Christian brotherhood and doomed to traipse the earth in search of a home. Everywhere the Gypsies traveled, the legends of their secret rituals and their mastery of unnatural arts preceded them.

It was said that Gypsies could understand the speech of horses, and could calm mares in labor with reassurance and advice. Gypsies buried their shadows in ground where they had been made unwelcome, to haunt the dreams of their oppressors; when Gypsy men died, their wild-haired women flung themselves into the grave to caress the coffin, and fought to remain there even as the

earth was shoveled in. The medieval church damned the ancestors of the Gypsies for having wrought the very nails that fixed Christ to the cross—but the Gypsies scoffed: If a Gypsy had made them, they said, the workmanship would have been so fine, and the nails so slim, that Christ would not even have felt them pass through his hands.

For it was true that the Gypsies had in their possession all manner of secret formulas for coaxing metals to perform fantastic feats. In particular, they fostered the power of iron to heal the sick and to ward off evil. Emblematic of this property was the horseshoe that hung above the doorway of every Romany caravan, to keep misfortune from sneaking in and infecting the family within. The story of how the simple "lucky horseshoe" came to be endowed with such supernatural strength was familiar to every Gypsy child from Naples to Vladivostok. The tale went this way:

Long ago there lived in the mountains four evil demons, known to the world as Bad Luck, Bad Health, Misery and Death. It was their mission and only pleasure to ambush innocent travelers and tear them to shreds in a frenzy of bloodlust. One night, after a riotous evening of drinking, dancing and song, a young Gypsy chieftain rode up into the hills to clear his head in the cool air. He had not gone far before the demon Bad Luck—left to watch for victims while his comrades snored—crashed out of the trees and lunged up the track, howling for

110

blood. The chieftain's horse reared in terror, turned and bolted back down the mountainside, its rider gripping tightly to its mane. At once Bad Luck gave chase. But as the horse fled clattering along the rocky path, one of its iron shoes flew off and smacked into Bad Luck's face, exactly between the eyes. With a dull thud that shook the mountain, the demon collapsed, dead as stone.

Bad Health, Misery and Death slept on. The cacophony of violence was lullaby to their ears. Hearing no sound of pursuit, the chieftain calmed his horse and returned to the stiffening corpse of Bad Luck. The prongs of the horseshoe were deeply embedded in his forehead. Wondering at the chance that had saved his life, the chieftain wrenched the shoe out and took it home to his camp; there, before the embers of a cooking fire, he told the tribe of his escape.

Shortly before dawn, the other three demons awoke feeling hungry; Bad Luck had brought them no meat. Ranging across the mountainside in search of their brother, they soon found the disfigured body on the track. Snatching birds from the trees and foxes from their lairs, the evil trio tortured them to tell the name of the man who had felled Bad Luck—and how he had done so.

While it was still dark, the avenging demons thundered into the Gypsy camp, bawling to the chieftain to show himself. Without hesitating, the young man threw open his caravan door; framed in light in the entrance, he boldly announced his presence. Even as he spoke, Bad Health, Misery and Death rushed snarling to rip him to pieces, but when they saw that the chieftain had nailed over his doorway the horseshoe that had killed Bad Luck, the demons quailed.

Remembering that the horse had yet three other shoes, the avengers slunk away into the night. Forever after, they padded in the tracks of Gypsy caravans, waiting for their revenge, and watching to spy out a doorway unguarded by the weapon that slew Bad Luck.

Gypsies, it was sometimes claimed, had been the first to master the science of metallurgy; but in truth, the art of the smith stretched further back in time even than the Romany race. Among every people, from the most sophisticated to the most barbaric, the blacksmith was credited with great powers. In Africa, a Wachaga smith took the greatest care with his simple tools, for if he pointed any of them at another human, that person was marked out for death. In the valleys of Southeast Asia, parents looked to blacksmiths to protect their newborn children from evil. The smith would forge a tiny iron ring to set around the baby's ankle. When the first, dangerous months had been successfully weathered, the infant would return to the forge and the ring would be removed.

Blacksmiths also possessed the art of healing; in their hands fire could cauterize, purify and invigorate. Paradoxically, as well as being sealers of wounds, they were weaponmakers. In the searing heat of their forges, smiths wrought suits of impenetrable chain mail, spiked maces, helmets of iron and shields of copper, and double-headed axes so strong they could hack the head off an elephant. They understood the ebb and flow of molten iron, and how to harness and condense its strength as steel.

Nowhere were these skills so crucial as in the forging of swords. If the steel was shoddy or hurriedly made, the blade would shatter when it struck against another that was not. The warrior's love of a fine sword was therefore the very stuff of jealous passion.

Some said the finest swords were the work of fairy smiths; others thought that the greatest blades came from the ancient race of dwarfs, working in underground forges. The magic of such beings produced swords that could warn their masters of impending danger or that would refuse to strike an unjust blow. The polished blades of certain brands could be used, like mirrors, for scrying. Arthur became King of England by effortlessly drawing from the bowels of a rock a sword that other men had failed to budge at all. It was Arthur, too, who rode to battle wielding bright Excalibur, most famous sword of all, given him at Merlin's bidding by the Lady of the Lake.

Other swords featured proudly in the unending struggle between mortals and the forces of darkness. When Beowulf plunged into a lake-bottom cave to fight the grisly mother of the monster Grendel, he took with him Hrunting, the mighty saber of herald Unferth. In the ensuing combat, Beowulf rammed Hrunt-ing into Grendel's mother. But the evil creature's blood was so corrosive that it melted the blade to a pool of black liquid. Undaunted, Beowulf snatched up another sword from the wall of the cave and attacked the vile beast once more. This weapon had been wrought long ago by giants—the most assiduous and talented of smiths; against such a powerful blade, the monster's body enjoyed no defense. With a hurricane of thrusts and hewing, Beowulf slew the foul ghoul, and returned triumphant to his people. Of Hrunting he spoke no unkind word. The sword had fought its best against a foe of unimaginable horror.

Of all the swords whose names were sung by poets of the Vikings, none was so vibrant with its own identity as Skofnung, the weapon of the warrior-king Hrolf Kraki. Skofnung had such a lust for blood that it would shriek in its scabbard at the sight of wounds, crying to be let out for carnage. When Kraki died, his subjects and descendants were too frightened of Skofnung to claim it as their own; instead, they buried the terrible sword with its master.

There Skofnung lay, untouched, for two long centuries, until a fearless warrior called Skeggi dug up the grave with his bare hands and wrested the weapon from the decomposed fist of the dead King. Skeggi's followers watched this desecration with alarm, convinced that Skofnung would turn on their leader and hack him to death. But Skofnung, it seemed, was content to be thus resurrected. In the peace of the grave there were no battles to be fought.

Swords were the proudest of weapons, and could have wills of their own. So one foolish Viking warrior found to his cost when he failed to treat a peerless blade with the respect it warranted.

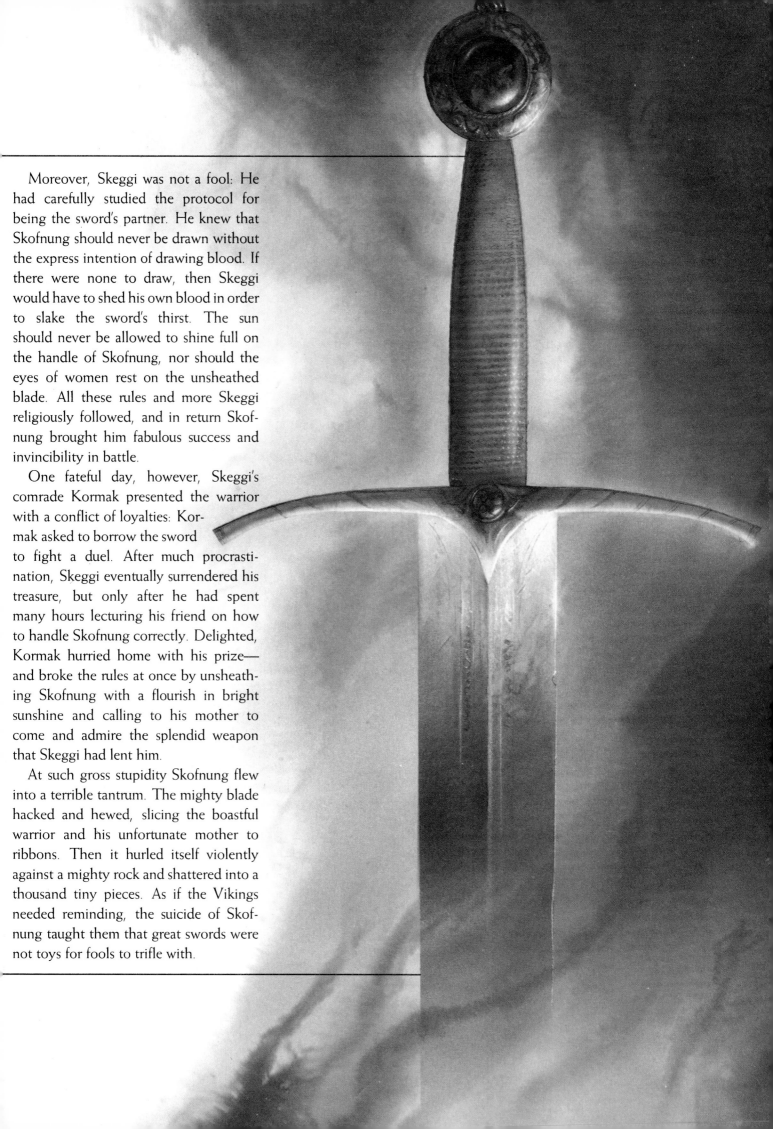

Moreover, Skeggi was not a fool: He had carefully studied the protocol for being the sword's partner. He knew that Skofnung should never be drawn without the express intention of drawing blood. If there were none to draw, then Skeggi would have to shed his own blood in order to slake the sword's thirst. The sun should never be allowed to shine full on the handle of Skofnung, nor should the eyes of women rest on the unsheathed blade. All these rules and more Skeggi religiously followed, and in return Skofnung brought him fabulous success and invincibility in battle.

One fateful day, however, Skeggi's comrade Kormak presented the warrior with a conflict of loyalties: Kormak asked to borrow the sword to fight a duel. After much procrastination, Skeggi eventually surrendered his treasure, but only after he had spent many hours lecturing his friend on how to handle Skofnung correctly. Delighted, Kormak hurried home with his prize—and broke the rules at once by unsheathing Skofnung with a flourish in bright sunshine and calling to his mother to come and admire the splendid weapon that Skeggi had lent him.

At such gross stupidity Skofnung flew into a terrible tantrum. The mighty blade hacked and hewed, slicing the boastful warrior and his unfortunate mother to ribbons. Then it hurled itself violently against a mighty rock and shattered into a thousand tiny pieces. As if the Vikings needed reminding, the suicide of Skofnung taught them that great swords were not toys for fools to trifle with.

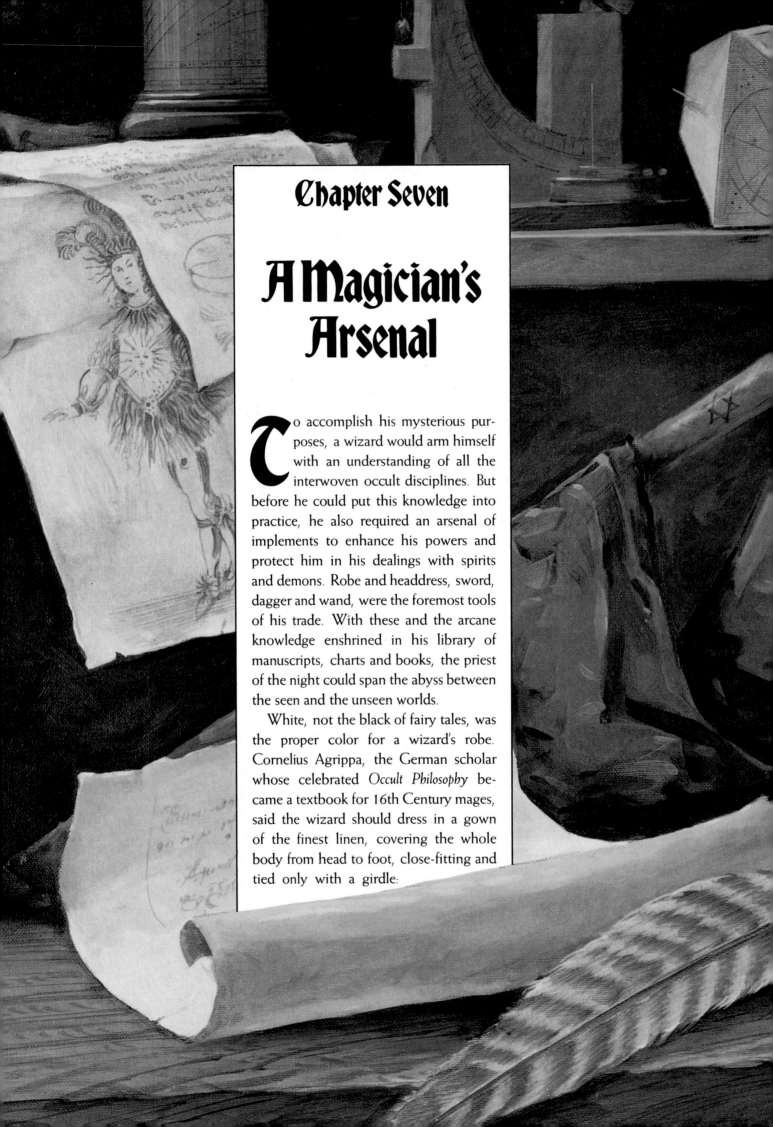

Chapter Seven

A Magician's Arsenal

To accomplish his mysterious purposes, a wizard would arm himself with an understanding of all the interwoven occult disciplines. But before he could put this knowledge into practice, he also required an arsenal of implements to enhance his powers and protect him in his dealings with spirits and demons. Robe and headdress, sword, dagger and wand, were the foremost tools of his trade. With these and the arcane knowledge enshrined in his library of manuscripts, charts and books, the priest of the night could span the abyss between the seen and the unseen worlds.

White, not the black of fairy tales, was the proper color for a wizard's robe. Cornelius Agrippa, the German scholar whose celebrated *Occult Philosophy* became a textbook for 16th Century mages, said the wizard should dress in a gown of the finest linen, covering the whole body from head to foot, close-fitting and tied only with a girdle:

Buckles and buttons would obstruct the free flow of supernatural energy. The headdress, whether tall or flat, pointed or round, should also be white, with YHVH, the Hebrew name of God, embroidered on the front. Both robe and headdress should be adorned with sacred emblems—stars, pentacles and circles.

Once equipped with headdress and robe, the wizard's most vital task was to forge a sword and dagger. This operation was best conducted when the moon was rising in the sphere of Jupiter, planet of good fortune and success. The mage would then burn incense of ambergris and peacocks' feathers, saffron, aloe wood, cedar and lapis lazuli—the scents associated with Jupiter—and chant in the name of God, heaven and the stars to infuse his weapons with mystic strength.

Only then could the wizard prepare his wand, the most precious of all the magic implements. A slim wooden rod, some twenty inches long, the wand was ideally cut from a solitary bush that had never fruited. On the first night of a new moon, in the hour before dawn, the magician should dip his knife in blood. Facing the eastern horizon, he should cut the shoot with a single stroke of his dagger, then peel its soft green bark in the first rays of the reborn sun. The three sacred instruments—sword, knife and wand—should then be wrapped in a silken cloth until they were required.

Delicate though it seemed, the slender wand was by far the most formidable weapon in the sorcerer's arsenal. With it he could summon spirits, cast spells or wreak destruction; he could make objects disappear, or reveal to the naked eye things that were otherwise invisible. If he were a beneficent practitioner, he might use the wand to liberate the victims of dark forces from the curses laid upon them, as did one nameless magician who wandered the seashores and valleys of Wales. This was how it happened:

The Welsh bards tell that, in the days of chivalry, a countryman named Einion was collecting berries for his wife Angharad in a wood near their cottage in Treveillir when he met a beautiful woman leading a black mare. He had never seen such a vision as this lady of the woods. Her black hair was combed in gleaming tresses, each held in place by a clasp of pearls; her red dress twinkled

A wizard prepared a wand of power by cutting a branch from a tree that had not yet fruited. To multiply the wand's magic, the blade that hewed it had to be steeped in blood.

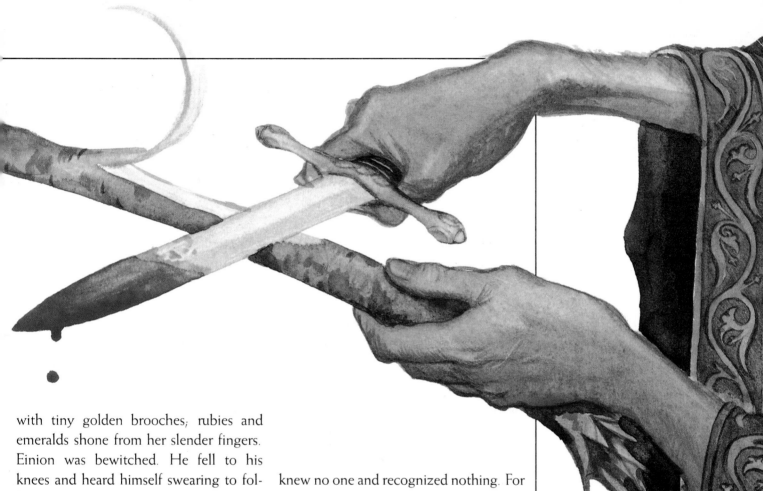

with tiny golden brooches; rubies and emeralds shone from her slender fingers. Einion was bewitched. He fell to his knees and heard himself swearing to follow her wherever she should lead.

But when Einion helped the lady to mount the black mare, he discovered that she had hooves instead of feet. He knew at once that he had fallen under the spell of a goblin, and begged to be released from his promise. But the lady of the woods was adamant. "You must follow me wherever I go," she commanded, "as long as my beauty shall last."

Then she took Einion to say farewell to Angharad, and laughed at his discomfiture when, in place of his young wife, he saw an aged crone, her body twisted, her face wrinkled.

Suddenly Einion found himself in a place he had never seen before, where he knew no one and recognized nothing. For what seemed like many years, he served the lady of the woods and followed wherever she led. Her beauty still beguiled him, but he knew he was under a spell, and each day he struggled to free himself from the illusion. Slowly his dreadful vision of Angharad faded, and he could again bring her youthful face to his mind's eye. But he still had no idea where he was, or how to return to his home.

One day, as Einion was exercising the black mare, he met a man in a white gown of the finest linen, riding a pure white stallion and carrying a slim white stick. They both dismounted and Einion asked the stranger if he had passed near Treveillir or heard news of Angharad. The stranger shook his head, but listened sympathetically. Soon Einion was telling

the whole story of his meeting with the lady of the woods, and his pledge to serve her for as long as her beauty should last. Then the horseman said, "If you truly wish to see your wife again, you must first face reality. Take this stick in your hand—and observe the beauty of the lady of the woods." Einion took the stick. At once a horrible goblin appeared before him, baying curses and howling threats of vengeance. But the stranger in white whipped his cloak around Einion to protect him, and the furious goblin sprang

Guided by a white-clad stranger, a Welsh peasant saw the true face of
the mistress who held him in thrall. A stroke of his benefactor's
wand exposed the fair lady as a monstrous goblin in disguise.

onto the black mare and galloped away.

The stranger took the stick again and pointed it at the ground. Suddenly, they were back at Treveillir, outside what Einion thought to be his cottage; but it seemed greatly changed—larger, more splendid, and surrounded with gardens and orchards. They were far from being the only visitors. The narrow lane, usually deserted, was full of bystanders peering over the wall; from the open windows of the house came laughter and the soft trills of a harp; and in an orchard beyond the house, pages dressed in livery were tethering a dozen magnificent horses— among them a handsome black mare.

The goblin, arch-manipulator of time and truth, had been busy. She had ridden straight to Angharad and, changed in appearance to a gallant knight, had won her over. Convincing Angharad that her husband was dead, the goblin-knight had even claimed her hand in marriage. And Angharad had been so impressed with the knight that she too had plunged into the world of illusion. The wedding celebrations had begun. But unlike Einion,

The woodlands of the old world abounded with caches of treasure, buried by long-dead sorcerers, thieves and Kings. Unknown or forgotten, the hiding-places remained inviolate, but a quivering switch in a diviner's hand could reveal their whereabouts.

Angharad had not seen the goblin's feet.

The two men pushed their way in through the crowd jostling in the lane and entered the house. In the kitchen, a dozen cooks were hard at work, roasting suckling pigs on a giant spit, simmering sauces in cast-iron pans, and piling salvers high with vegetables and exotic fruits. Butlers with silver ewers hurried through the halls, filling goblets for everyone that they passed. Einion and the stranger in white followed the strains of music and squeezed into the best room of the house, where Angharad and the goblin-knight sat on a velvet couch, listening to a courtier plucking a golden harp.

Then Einion stepped forward and offered to play an air that he knew was Angharad's favorite. She looked at him and saw only an old man, bent and weary, with watery eyes and withered jowls. She watched curiously as Einion sat down at the harp and tuned it, then plucked the strings with tremulous fingers. A scrap of memory flickered across her mind, but was quickly banished. By the time Einion played the last notes of the melody, he knew that Angharad was lost to him.

The goblin-knight held her in his arms and caressed her cheek. She gazed lovingly into his eyes. Then the white-clad stranger leaned forward and placed the white stick into Angharad's hand. Instantly she saw the handsome knight transformed into the most hideous demon, and she shrieked in a frenzy of fear until her voice gave out and her body slumped to the floor. When Angharad revived, the room was as it always had been, with the old wooden harp set by the window, a small peat fire burning in the hearth and Einion snoring beside her on the settle. Of the goblin-knight and the white-clad stranger who had broken the spell, there was no trace.

Many writers on the magic arts recorded that the best wands were made from hazel wood, and this tradition may date as far back as biblical times. According to Hebrew sages, the rod of Moses was cut from a hazel tree in the Garden of Eden; with it the leader of the Israelites was able to divide the waters of the Red Sea and to strike water from a desert rock.

The hazel's botanical attributes may have played some part in winning the tree its unique standing. Because it flowered at the end of winter, the Germans regarded it as an emblem of immortality, while English farmers picked branches bearing catkins—also known as lambs' tails—to encourage their sheep during the lambing season. Hazelnuts were widely held to symbolize love and nuptial happiness.

But botany cannot explain the long-held belief, recorded by the 16th Century scholar Agricola, for example, that a forked wand could be used to find underground springs, coal and precious metal, even buried treasure. For many centuries, diviners known as dowsers detected the vibrations emitted by these subterranean elements by walking with a hazel rod held out in front of them. When the rod passed over water or metal, it would dip and twist in the dowser's hands.

Hazel was not the only tree endowed with such mysterious qualities. Alder,

oak and apple twigs could all produce the same effects. Blackthorn was favored in Ireland, especially if cut from an isolated bush concealed in a moorland hollow, which might be a fairies' trysting-place. Some Welsh dowsers preferred to use yew instead of hazel. In this they followed the custom of their country's wizards, who chose the yew tree to supply wands. So powerful was this wood that even a wand prepared by the uninitiated could sometimes have marvelous effects.

According to one celebrated legend, a Welsh cattle-drover named Dafyd Meirig cut a yew switch at dawn one day to use as a goad while driving his beasts across country to London's Smithfield Market. A week later, his livestock sold, he strolled across London Bridge, swinging his stick and admiring the view. Dafyd was so taken by the sights of the great city that he did not notice the stick twisting as he crossed the river. But an English wizard, passing by, observed it, and asked

In a subterranean cavern, one thousand sleeping heroes guarded a heap of ancient gold. With the aid of a magician, a cattle-drover penetrated the sanctuary and helped himself to treasure.

Dafyd where he had found the switch.

When the wizard heard that the drover had cut the rod himself, he told Dafyd that such a potent tree must draw its strength from forces beneath the earth. Only gold and silver could yield such energy, he declared. And he promised Dafyd unlimited riches if he would lead him to the yew tree from which it came.

Dafyd Meirig agreed. Together they made the journey back to Wales, finally arriving at the great hill of Craig-y-Dinas, the Rock of the Fortress, beneath which, it was said, King Arthur and his knights awaited the call to fight again.

There on the hillside, close to a fork in the drove road, Dafyd and the wizard found the yew. It was old, but scarcely larger than a bush, bent low by gales, gripping the stony soil with gnarled and twisting roots.

That night was propitious for their search since the moon was rising in the sphere of Jupiter. In the hour before dawn, the two men dug around the yew tree's roots until they found a heavy oblong slate. Beneath it yawned a narrow staircase, and at its foot a winding passageway led deep into the hillside. The two men followed it for several hundred feet, until the wizard touched Dafyd's sleeve and pointed out a heavy golden bell hanging at the end of the passage. They ducked beneath it and entered a cavern, lighted with an eerie glow.

Before them a thousand warriors lay sleeping in a giant circle, shoulder to shoulder, swords in hand. At the center a King—who must have been Arthur—sat entranced and motionless, a massive broadsword in his hands. Dafyd's eyes slowly took in the scene. Then he realized that the strange light, which had seemed to come from a fire behind the King, was cast by two great heaps of gold. The magician whispered to Dafyd that he could claim as much treasure as he could carry, and the Welshman quickly stuffed his shirt and coat with gold.

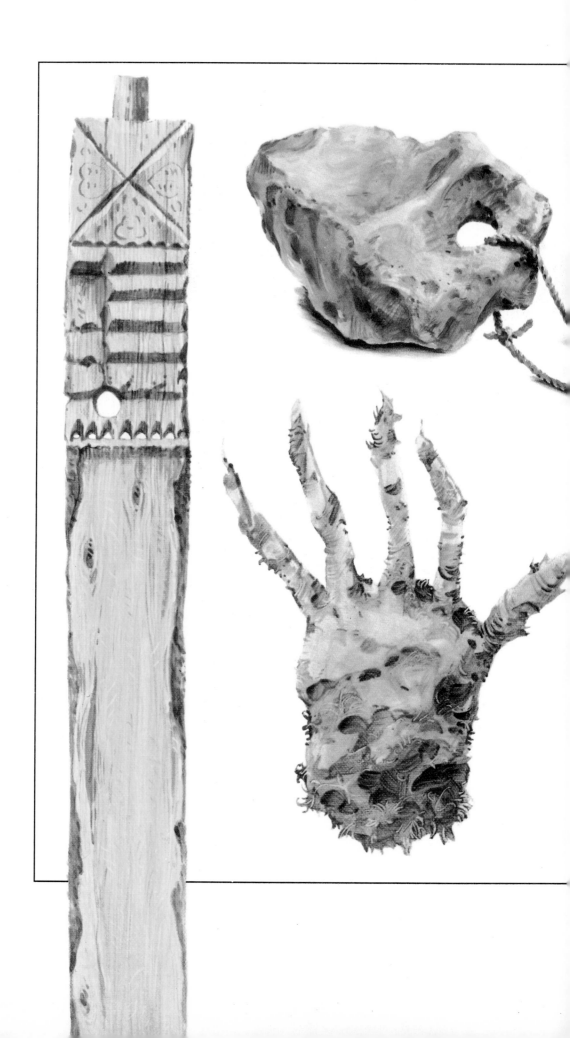

Defenses against spiritual assault

In the dangerous times when demons lurked in the shadows by day and sought to enter mortal dwellings at night, people used what tools they could to shelter themselves and their loved ones from harm. A thorough versing in the lore of charms, the traditional antidotes to evil, provided the best hope of success.

In cases of supernatural assault, the weakest points of any home were its apertures—doors, windows, and especially the wide chimneys. Such inviting entrances needed constant protection. A simple wooden post, carved with bands and crosses, might be set up to guard the hearth against the incursions of witches. The color red was also effective against their malice; bundles of twigs from the scarlet-berried rowan were tied into a cross with crimson thread to guard a door or window.

Nature offered numerous such antidotes to evil. A chance-found stone with a hole worn through it brought certain luck, for example, particularly if the finder tied a key or some other iron object to it. Brilliant kingfisher feathers were also sought out; folded in fresh linen, they would keep the cloth safe from decay even as they kept the owner safe from baleful magic.

Other devices offered personal security against the evil eye. Because an open palm was the sovereign remedy, on Midsummer Eve peasants searched out wild orchid roots that mimicked the shape of an uncurled fist. When traveling, riders sought to assure their safe arrival by embellishing their horses' bridles with brightly-polished brasses that reflected ill-will back toward its source. Crescent shapes were particularly favored for this: Bearing the form of the waxing moon, their influence was especially benign.

Then they left as they had come, taking great care to avoid ringing the bell.

It was almost dawn when they emerged on the hillside and heaved the slate back over the narrow opening. The Englishman told Dafyd that he might return as often as he wished to collect more gold, but warned him never to disturb the bell. Then the wizard cut a slim, straight shoot from the blasted yew, and peeled its green bark with a small dagger. As the first rays of the reborn sun lanced over the horizon, the two men parted.

Dafyd Meirig grew fat and lazy on the proceeds of that night, and years passed before he found either the need or the courage to enter the cave alone. But finally greed and curiosity overcame him. Taking a stout sack, he walked in darkness across the bleak hillside to the yew tree and pushed aside the stone. Moments later, he had stuffed the sack with gold and hoisted it onto his shoulders, scarcely glancing at King Arthur and the sleeping warriors. Dafyd stooped beneath the heavy bell. But he could not bend low enough. The sack of gold struck it and the bell's ear-splitting chime brought every warrior instantly to his feet.

Mailed fists seized the drover and beat him mercilessly before throwing him empty-handed back into the night. After that, Dafyd never again dared venture onto the Craig-y-Dinas. He told his story often, however, and many people searched for the slate beneath the yew, but always in vain.

To an initiate in the occult arts, this tale reaffirmed the fact that magic implements could draw strength from the dead. By the same principle, bones could hold great power. They were worn as talismans, ground up for consumption in curative potions, employed as tools in curses and conjuring. And no wizard's workshop was complete without a polished skull grinning out from the clutter of scrying glasses, medicine jars, wands and incunabula. For sorcerers of a moralizing bent, the relics provided a reminder of humankind's inescapable and universal destiny, while practitioners with a more pragmatic turn of mind used skulls as mortars, mixing bowls or caldrons. But every wizard knew that skulls had the power to deflect evil, keeping watch through eyeless sockets and blocking demons with a barricade of bone.

In the magician's arsenal, such defensive shields were as important as wands or spell books. Physical safety, even survival, could depend on them. The invocation of spirits was always a dangerous enterprise, for denizens of the demonic realm were reluctant servants and untrustworthy collaborators. No wonderworker, however sure of his skills, was naive enough to trust them. Before calling up these volatile powers from the darkness, the initiate had to take precautions. Following directions laid down in the grimoires—the old handbooks of sorcery—he drew a magic circle on the floor of his chamber, or on the earth itself if he worked outdoors. Its purpose was to form a boundary that no spirit dared cross.

The grimoires differed in their instructions. Some enjoined the practitioner to draw the figure on the ground with the point of a magic sword or dagger; others exhorted the use of vermilion paint, a color demons were thought to abhor. The circle had to consist of two concentric rings, the space between them densely filled with inscribed words of power and pots of devil-deterring herbs.

Safe within its circumference, a wizard could summon up even the most malevolent entities and command them without danger to himself. But if he stepped outside the circle, or even thrust an arm or leg over the line by accident, no formula could save him. His death would be violent, swift and explosive, and his suffering would endure beyond the grave.

Only one man in all the long history of magic had been able to consort with demons without such defenses. This was the mighty monarch Solomon, whose dominions, so it was whispered, extended beyond the lands of the Hebrews to encompass the spirit world itself.

The secret lore of this master magician flowed like an underground river. Arab sages and Jewish mystics preserved anecdotes of his power that did not find their way into the more conventional chronicles. One of these concerned an extraordinary trial, held in Solomon's palace at Jerusalem. The plaintiff was a poor widow, the charge was theft, and the defendants were the four winds.

It pleased the King to hold a daily audience in his palace. On one spring afternoon, the great hall was packed with petitioners: farmers quarreling over boundaries between their olive groves, heirs disputing the terms of a will, scholars anxious for the King's adjudication on some point of law. Palace servants opened the high windows, hoping the breezes might dilute the choking cloud of stale perfumes, sweat and exhaled onions.

The crowd grew impatient, pushing ever closer to the throne where the great Solomon sat in splendor, surrounded by the high priests of his temple, awesome

Skulls of the dead, circles adorned with occult symbols, formulas for devil-raising, were the sorcerer's stock-in-trade. But even the most skilled adepts used these tools warily, for they knew themselves to be playing with cosmic fire.

So mighty a mage was King Solomon that he did not fear to put even the
forces of nature on trial. When a widow complained of maltreatment,
the monarch summoned all four winds to answer the charges.

in their horned headdresses. The King leaned forward to catch the stammers of an awestruck supplicant. But a sudden commotion at the rear of the great hall made listening impossible. A small figure slipped through the crowd like wind through a wheat field.

Solomon's face darkened when he discovered that the interloper was his twelve-year-old son, whom the tale-tellers named Absalom. The boy announced that he had discovered a terrible crime, which had to be avenged at once. The King commanded Absalom to hold his peace until the man before him had had his say. The boy fumed and fidgeted, weeping tears of outrage. Finally, at Solomon's nod, Absalom approached the throne and told his story. He had spent that morning in the study-house, learning the portion of the law concerned with justice for the needy. On his way home he heard weeping, and followed the sound to the mouth of a muddy alleyway. A woman, dressed in ragged mourning, crouched on the ground, sobbing into an empty bowl. Her skirt, her sandaled feet and the mud she sat in were spattered with flour. Absalom lifted up the widow and hurried her to his father's palace, ignoring all her protestations and promising she would find justice at his father's court. Even now, she waited at the door of the great hall. The King beckoned her

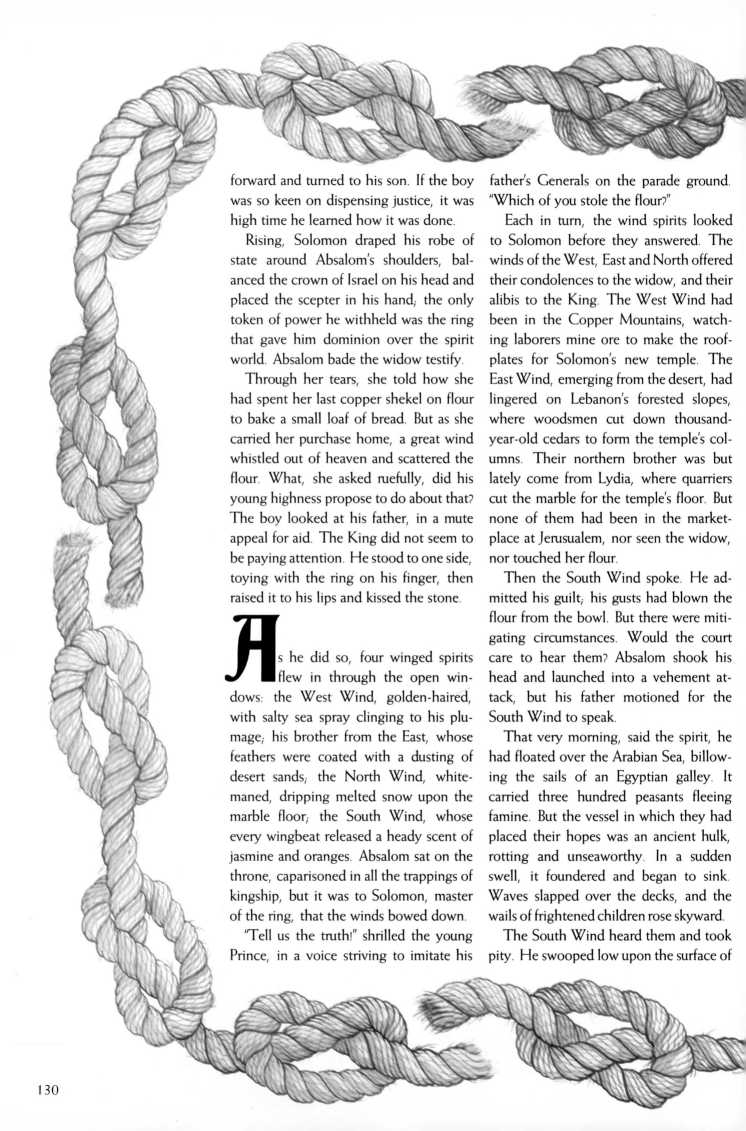

forward and turned to his son. If the boy was so keen on dispensing justice, it was high time he learned how it was done.

Rising, Solomon draped his robe of state around Absalom's shoulders, balanced the crown of Israel on his head and placed the scepter in his hand; the only token of power he withheld was the ring that gave him dominion over the spirit world. Absalom bade the widow testify.

Through her tears, she told how she had spent her last copper shekel on flour to bake a small loaf of bread. But as she carried her purchase home, a great wind whistled out of heaven and scattered the flour. What, she asked ruefully, did his young highness propose to do about that? The boy looked at his father, in a mute appeal for aid. The King did not seem to be paying attention. He stood to one side, toying with the ring on his finger, then raised it to his lips and kissed the stone.

As he did so, four winged spirits flew in through the open windows: the West Wind, golden-haired, with salty sea spray clinging to his plumage; his brother from the East, whose feathers were coated with a dusting of desert sands; the North Wind, white-maned, dripping melted snow upon the marble floor; the South Wind, whose every wingbeat released a heady scent of jasmine and oranges. Absalom sat on the throne, caparisoned in all the trappings of kingship, but it was to Solomon, master of the ring, that the winds bowed down.

"Tell us the truth!" shrilled the young Prince, in a voice striving to imitate his father's Generals on the parade ground. "Which of you stole the flour?"

Each in turn, the wind spirits looked to Solomon before they answered. The winds of the West, East and North offered their condolences to the widow, and their alibis to the King. The West Wind had been in the Copper Mountains, watching laborers mine ore to make the roofplates for Solomon's new temple. The East Wind, emerging from the desert, had lingered on Lebanon's forested slopes, where woodsmen cut down thousand-year-old cedars to form the temple's columns. Their northern brother was but lately come from Lydia, where quarriers cut the marble for the temple's floor. But none of them had been in the marketplace at Jerusualem, nor seen the widow, nor touched her flour.

Then the South Wind spoke. He admitted his guilt; his gusts had blown the flour from the bowl. But there were mitigating circumstances. Would the court care to hear them? Absalom shook his head and launched into a vehement attack, but his father motioned for the South Wind to speak.

That very morning, said the spirit, he had floated over the Arabian Sea, billowing the sails of an Egyptian galley. It carried three hundred peasants fleeing famine. But the vessel in which they had placed their hopes was an ancient hulk, rotting and unseaworthy. In a sudden swell, it foundered and began to sink. Waves slapped over the decks, and the wails of frightened children rose skyward.

The South Wind heard them and took pity. He swooped low upon the surface of the sea, gathered all his strength and blew the craft to shore. As it ran aground, the ship broke up beyond repair, but none of the souls it carried perished. So vigorously did the South Wind perform this act of mercy that its strength was felt as far as Jerusalem. The blast that saved three hundred lives was the blast that stole the widow's flour.

His face crimson, the Prince slipped off the throne and handed back the tokens of power to Solomon. The King ordered his treasurer to compensate the widow for her loss with one hundred golden shekels. This done, he turned to the South Wind and held out the hand that wore the ring of power. The spirit kneeled before it to receive the monarch's blessing. Then he soared out through the open window and vanished into the sky. But for many days thereafter, the fragrance of southern blooms and spices lingered in the hall.

Solomon, the greatest magician of his own or any age, could command the winds by a touch of his ring and a simple word of power, confident of unquestioning obedience. But lesser practitioners also sought dominion over the elements. The witches who dwelled in the wild seafaring lands of Europe's northern verges were famed and feared for their weatherwork. Shetland sailors climbed dank stone staircases in the port of Lerwick to buy fair winds tied up in string from certain old women. Estonian peasants cast a baleful eye on their Finnish neighbors, whose wizards were said to send foul weather over the border. These sorcerers trapped the wind with three different knots: Untying the first produced a breeze, the second unleashed a gale, the third sent forth a hurricane.

Many a ship's crew, surprised by the sudden arrival of foul weather, wondered what onshore enemy wished them ill. They knew that Scottish warlocks, on receipt of a fat purse, were more than willing to summon up a storm. If, by chance, the winds did not obey them in their evil ploys, these wizards would not scruple to subvert the sea itself. A dish set afloat in a pail of water could be upset and sunk by dint of spoken spells. And at the precise moment that the bowl turned over in the pail of water, a ship would capsize, somewhere out at sea.

In skilled hands, such humble utensils could be as efficacious as the arcane apparatus of Agrippa and his ilk. A true initiate into the secret arts understood that all the world was a workshop, full of untapped potencies and untested tools. Wands and circles, skulls and rings, knots and spells, were but the best-known keys to unlock the door into a different, and dangerous, universe.

The War between Light and Darkness

As old as time, and as implacable, the war between good and evil magic never ceased. In the earliest days, the hierophants of rival cults called upon their shadowy gods to outdo each other's miracles; forever after, evil sorcerers tested their mettle against adepts who worked their wonders for the good of humankind.

Jewish storytellers of Eastern Europe spoke of a sage named Rabbi Israel, who conducted a trial of strength against an emissary from hell.

On a long journey, the Rabbi and his disciples paused for the night at an inn. On entering, they found it empty, although its tables were covered with embroidered cloths and set with goblets and silver platters as if for a feast. Then they heard sobbing from the kitchen. There the innkeeper and his family sat weeping around a small, but empty, coffin.

The host explained that the feast was to celebrate the birth of his son. But his wife had borne two boys before; each one had died on the eve of the festivities. This time, he was ready for the worst: The tiny casket awaited its occupant.

The Rabbi mused awhile; he ordered candles to be lit around the baby's cradle and a sack placed behind his head. He and two pupils settled down to watch.

An hour after midnight, the candles wavered. A cat glided silently toward the cradle, its presence betrayed only by two green eyes shining out of the gloom.

With a sudden hiss, the feline bunched its shanks and sprang. But at that very instant, it met the Rabbi's gaze. The cat froze in midair, then fell into the open sack. Swiftly, the students pulled the drawstrings to imprison the creature. The Rabbi, laughing softly, reached for a stick and belabored the cat with all his might. At last, when his arm was tired, he opened the window and emptied the sack's shrieking contents into the night.

The next day, the feast was held amid much rejoicing. But strangely, the lord of the manor, who was to have been the guest of honor, was absent. Bearing a gift of festive cake, the Rabbi inquired at the manor house, where he found the man lying in bed, bruised all over. The two recognized each other instantly. The lord's eyes glowed green; hissing furiously, he challenged the Rabbi to a test of supernatural strength.

The next morning, a platform was raised in the nobleman's courtyard and a huge furnace erected. Seeing this, the Rabbi smiled, summoned his students to him and traced two concentric circles in the earth around them.

His opponent fired the furnace and flung open the doors. A multitude of wild beasts leaped out, sprang at the Rabbi, but could not pass the circles. Again the lord opened the doors. This time the sun dimmed, the air became dark, and the furnace spewed forth creatures of the night. Some bony and clad in rags, some plump and blind like huge maggots, they advanced on the circles, which wavered as if the earth quaked beneath. But the Rabbi raised

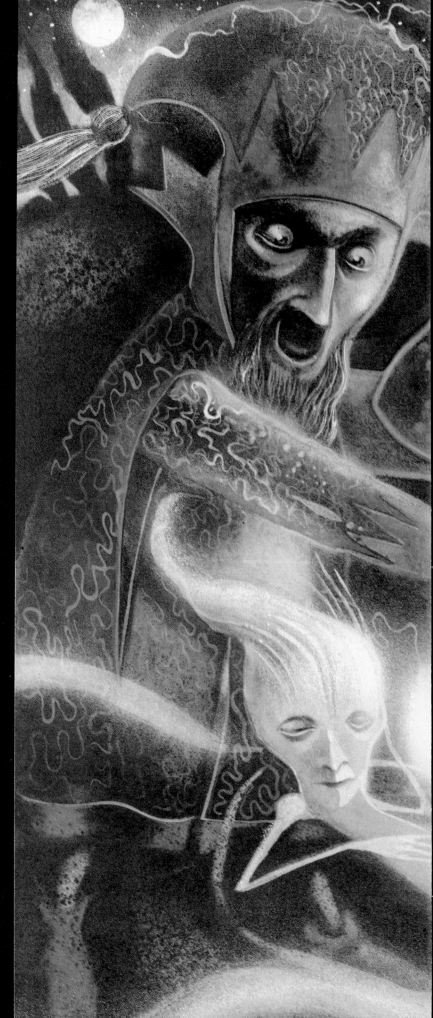

his hand and muttered prayers that
caused the attackers to vanish.

For two days and nights the battle
raged on. Again and again the sorcerer
opened his furnace doors; each onslaught
was more terrifying than the last. Even
the dead were called back from their
graves, but although the circles quivered
so much that they threatened to break,
the Rabbi and his students remained safe.

On the third day the nobleman began to weaken, and he resolved to
bring out his most powerful ally.
He ordered his serfs to stoke the
furnace until it could take no more.
Then, when the flames were at their
height, he walked into the fire and summoned the Devil. The pair embraced,
and such was the heat of their malevolence that the very grass about the Rabbi's feet began to smolder. Replete with
power, the sorcerer strode out of the
furnace, seized a pig from one of the
villagers, and dashed it to the ground.
Under his evil gaze, its belly broke
and where its entrails split, the ground
opened in a dark chasm.

Out of the crevice there arose an army
of monstrous creatures, breathing fire.
Slithering and crawling, they rushed at
the Rabbi and burst through the outer
circle. The scorched earth cracked and

inner circle started to crumble. But
Rabbi called his pupils close and,
ing his arm, began to utter words of
y and power. With each syllable, the
tures diminished, sinking back into
dirt from which they had arisen.
e earth closed, and all became still. .
xhausted, the lord fell to his knees by
useless furnace and begged to be de-
yed, for he was beaten. The Rabbi
ked down on his adversary with con-
pt and replied, "I shall not destroy
." Then he ordered the broken man
kneel and raise his eyes to heaven.
e lord did as he was bid, and a low
an escaped his lips as he saw two
k specks in the sky. The specks
w larger and larger, until at last they
ame visible as a pair of eagles.

wooping down, they sank their
talons in the face of the kneeling
sorcerer. As he screamed in terror,
they worked their hooked beaks
into his eye sockets, plucked out
eyes, and disappeared into the sky.
sfied with the punishment, the Rabbi
d his disciples to him, and the group
inued on its travels once more. Be-
them, they left the sorcerer-lord,
led, belittled, bereft of power, and
quished by the might of faith and the
of virtuous magic.

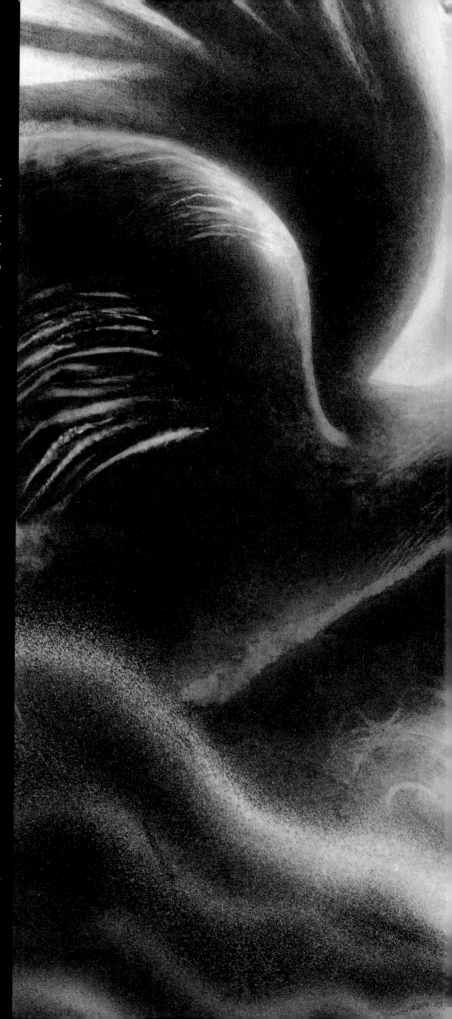

Acknowledgments

The editors wish to thank the following persons for their help in the preparation of this volume: Guy Andrews, London; Susie Dawson, London; Fergus Fleming, London; John Gaisford, London; Nick Growse, Bury St. Edmunds, Suffolk, England; Alan Lothian, Anghiari, Italy; Simone Mühlen, German Institute Library, London; Venetia Newall, London; Robin Olson, London; Deborah Thompson, London; Hanna Tourmouche, German Institute Library, London; Waltraud Vogler, London.

Picture Credits

The sources for the illustrations in this book are shown below.

Cover: Artwork by John Howe. 1-5: Artwork by Giles Waring. 6-7: Artwork by Malcolm Chandler. 8-13: Artwork by Tony Smith. 15: Artwork by Max Schindler. 16: Artwork by Nick Harris. 18: Artwork by John Watkiss. 21-22: Artwork by Giles Waring. 23: Artwork by John Watkiss. 24-25: Artwork by David O'Connor. 26: Artwork by Susan Gallagher. 27-29: Courtesy The Mary Evans Picture Library, London. 30-31: Artwork by Gillian Tyler. 32-33: Artwork by Roy Coombes. 34-35: Artwork by Cathy Shuttleworth. 37: William Blake, courtesy The Tate Gallery, London. 39: Dante Gabriel Rossetti, courtesy The Fitzwilliam Museum, Cambridge, England. 40-41: Artwork by Philip Argent. 42, bottom: Based on an engraving by Albrecht Dürer, courtesy The Mary Evans Picture Library, London. 42-43: Artwork by Tony Smith (top), Shirley Cullum (center) and Max Schindler (bottom right). 44-45: Artwork by David Bergen. 46: Courtesy The Mary Evans Picture Library, London. 47: Artwork by John Sibbick. 48-49: Artwork by Alan Baker. 50-51: Artwork by John Sibbick. 52-53: Artwork by Shirley Cullum. 54-55: Artwork by Ian Miller. 56-57: Artwork by Nick Harris. 58-59: Artwork by Pam Masco. 60-61: Artwork by Malcolm Chandler. 63-65: Artwork by Mark Langeneckert. 66-67: Artwork by Charles Raymond. 68: Artwork by Tim Pearce. 70-71: Artwork by Anita Kunz. 72: Artwork by Graham Ward. 73: Artwork by Malcolm Chandler. 74-79: Artwork by Gary Kelley. 80-81: Artwork by Jenny Tylden-Wright. 82: Artwork by Martin Knowelden. 85: Artwork by David O'Connor. 86-87: Artwork by Fataneh Ramazani and John Howe. 88-89: Artwork by Lynne Dennis. 90-93: Artwork by Susan Gallagher. 94-99: Artwork by George Sharp. 100-101: Artwork by David O'Connor. 102-103: Artwork by Alan Baker. 104-107: Artwork by Barbara Loftus. 109: William Holman Hunt, courtesy The Bridgeman Art Library, London. 110: Artwork by Ed Dovey. 113: Artwork by John Howe. 114-115: Artwork by Malcolm Chandler. 116-117: Artwork by Giles Waring. 118-119: Artwork by David Bergen. 120-121: Artwork by Niall Harding. 122-123: Artwork by John Howe. 124-125: Artwork by Caroline Holmes Smith. 126: Artwork by Tim Pearce. 128-129: Artwork by Nick Harris. 130-131: Artwork by Philip Argent. 132-139: Artwork by Graham Ward. 144: Artwork by Giles Waring.

Bibliography

Aelian, *On the Characteristics of Animals*. Transl. by A. F. Scholfield. London: Heinemann, 1959.

Aldington, Richard, and Delano Ames, transls., *New Larousse Encyclopedia of Mythology*. London: The Hamlyn Publishing Group, 1985.*

Arnason, Jón., *Icelandic Legends*. Transl. by George E. J. Powell and Eiríkur Magnússon. London: Longmans, Green, 1866.

Aubrey, John, *Miscellanies upon Various Subjects*. London: John Russell Smith, 1857.

Baring-Gould, S., *Curious Myths of the Middle Ages*. London: Rivingtons, 1866.

Barker, Andrew, ed., *Greek Musical Writings, the Musician and his Art*. Vol. 1. Cambridge: Cambridge University Press, 1984.

Bayley, Harold, *The Lost Language of Symbolism*. Vol. 1. London: Williams and Norgate, 1912.

Bermant, Chaim, *The Walled Garden*. London: Weidenfeld & Nicolson, 1974.

Brewer's Dictionary of Phrase and Fable. Rev. by Ivor H. Evans. London: Cassell, 1970.

Briggs, Katherine:
The Anatomy of Puck. London: Routledge & Kegan Paul, 1959.
A Dictionary of Fairies. Harmondsworth, England: Penguin Books, 1977.*
The Witch Figure. Ed. by Venetia Newall. London: Routledge & Kegan Paul, 1973.

Buffum, W. Arnold, *The Tears of the Heliades, or Amber as a Gem*. London: Sampson Low, Marston, 1898.

Burland, C. A., *The Magical Arts*. London: Arthur Barker, 1966.*

Butler, Elizabeth M., *Ritual Magic*. Cambridge: Cambridge University Press, 1949.

Campbell, John Gregorson, collected by, *Superstitions of the Highlands & Islands of Scotland*. Glasgow: James MacLehose and Sons, 1900.*

Cavendish, Richard:
The Black Arts. London: Routledge & Kegan Paul, 1967.*
Ed., *Man, Myth and Magic*. 11 vols. New York: Marshall Cavendish, 1983.*

Christian, Paul, *The History and Practice of Magic*. Transl. by James Kirkup and Julian Shaw. 2 vols. London: Forge Press, 1952.*

Cirlot, J. E., *A Dictionary of Symbols*. London: Routledge & Kegan Paul, 1962.

Copeman, W. S. C., *Doctors and Disease in Tudor Times*. London: Dawson's of Pall Mall, 1960.

Davidson, H. R. Ellis:
Gods and Myths of Northern Europe. Harmondsworth, England: Penguin Books, 1964.
The Sword in Anglo-Saxon England. Oxford: Clarendon Press, 1962.

Dawson, W. R., *Magician and Leech*. London: Methuen, 1930.

de Becker, *The Understanding of Dreams*. Transl. by Michael Heron. London: George Allen & Unwin, 1968.

de Givry, Grillot, *Witchcraft, Magic and Alchemy*. Transl. by J. Courtenay Locke. New York: Dover Publications, 1971.*

de Rola, Stanislas Klossowski, *Alchemy: The Secret Art*. New York: Avon Books, 1973.

Dodd, A. H., *Life in Elizabethan England*. Ed. by Peter Quennell. London: B. T. Batsford, 1967.

Dunbabin, T. J., *The Western Greeks*. Oxford: Clarendon Press, 1948.

Eliade, Mircea:
The Forge and the Crucible. Transl. by Stephen Corrin. London: Rider, 1962.
A History of Religious Ideas. Transl. by Willard R. Trask. London: Collins, 1979.
Patterns in Comparative Religion. Transl. by Rosemary Sheed.

London: Sheed and Ward, 1958.

Elliott, Ralph W. V., *Runes*. Manchester: Manchester University Press, 1959.

Elworthy, Frederick Thomas, *The Evil Eye*. London: John Murray, 1895.

Erman, Adolf, *The Literature of the Ancient Egyptians*. Transl. by Aylward M. Blackman. London: Methuen, 1927.

Evans, Joan, *Magical Jewels of the Middle Ages and the Renaissance*. Oxford: Clarendon Press, 1922.*

Evans-Wentz, W. Y., *The Fairy-Faith in Celtic Countries*. Gerrards Cross, Bucks., England: Colin Smythe, 1977.

Farr, Florence, *Egyptian Magic*. Wellingborough, Northants., England: The Aquarian Press, 1982.

Folkard, Richard, *Plant Lore, Legends and Lyrics*. London: Sampson Low, Marston, Searle & Rivington, 1884.*

Foote, Peter, and David M. Wilson, *The Viking Achievement*. London: Sidgwick & Jackson, 1980.

Frazer, Sir James George, *The Golden Bough*. London: Macmillan, 1967.

Freden, Gustaf, *Orpheus and the Goddess of Nature*. Göteborg, Sweden: Elanders Boktryckeri Akmebolag, 1958.

Frith, Henry, *Chiromancy, or the Science of Palmistry*. London: George Routledge and Sons, 1888.*

Gaster, Theodor H., *Myth, Legend and Custom in the Old Testament*. London: Macmillan, 1918.*

Graves, Robert, *The Greek Myths*. 2 vols. Harmondsworth, England: Penguin Books, 1955.

Green, Roger Lancelyn, selected and retold by, *Tales of Ancient Egypt*. Harmondsworth, England.: Penguin Books, 1971.*

Grigson, Geoffrey, *A Herbal of all Sorts*. London: Phoenix House, 1959.

Guerber, H. A., *Legends of the Rhine*. New York: A. S. Barnes, 1895.*

Guillaume, Alfred, *Prophecy and

Divination*. London: Hodder & Stoughton, 1938.

Hart, George, *A Dictionary of Egyptian Gods and Goddesses*. London: Routledge & Kegan Paul, 1986.

Hole, Christina, *English Folklore*. New York: Charles Scribner's Sons, 1940.

Homer, *The Odyssey*. Transl. by S. H. Butcher and A. Lang. London: Macmillan, 1903.*

Howes, Michael, *Amulets*. London: Robert Hale, 1975.*

Hueffer, Oliver Madox, *The Book of Witches*. London: Eveleigh Nash, 1908.

Hunt, Robert, collected and ed. by, *Popular Romances of the West of England*. London: Chatto & Windus, 1930.*

Ingoldsby, Thomas, *Ingoldsby Legends*. London: Richard Bentley, 1840.*

Jones, William:
Credulities Past and Present. London: Chatto & Windus, 1880.
Finger-Ring Lore. London: Chatto & Windus, 1877.
History and Mystery of Precious Stones. London: Richard Bentley and Son, 1880.*

Kaplan, Stuart R., *The Classical Tarot*. Wellingborough, Northants., England: The Aquarian Press, 1972.

Katan, Norma Jean, with Barbara Mintz, *Hieroglyphs*. London: British Museum Publications, 1985.*

Kirby, W. F., transl., *Kalevala, the Land of the Heroes*. London: The Athlone Press, 1985.*

Kittredge, George Lyman, *Witchcraft in Old and New England*. Cambridge, Mass.: Harvard University Press, 1929.*

Kozminsky, Isidore, *The Magic and Science of Jewels and Stones*. New York: G. P. Putnam's Sons, 1922.

Krappe, Alexander Haggerty, *The Science of Folklore*. London: Methuen, 1930.

Kunz, George Frederick:
The Curious Lore of Precious Stones. Philadelphia: J. B. Lippincott, 1913.*
The Magic of Jewels and Charms. Philadelphia: J. B. Lippincott, 1915.*

Lawrence, Eugene, *The Science of Palmistry*. London: Kegan Paul, Trench, Trubner, 1905.

Lawrence, Robert Means, *The Magic of the Horse-Shoe*. Boston: Houghton, Mifflin, 1899.

Leach, Maria, ed., *Funk & Wagnalls Standard Dictionary of Folklore, Mythology and Legend*. San Francisco: Harper & Row, 1984.*

Le Braz, *The Celtic Legend of the Beyond*. Transl. by Derek Bryce. Lampeter, Dyfed, Wales: Llanerch Enterprises, 1986.*

Lehner, Ernst, and Johanna Lehner, *Picture Book of Devils, Demons and Witchcraft*. New York: Dover Publications, 1971.

Levin, Meyer, *Classic Hassidic Tales*. New York: The Citadel Press, 1966.*

Leyel, C. F., *The Magic of Herbs*. London: Jonathan Cape, 1926.

MacKenzie, Norman, *Dreams and Dreaming*. London: Aldus Books, 1965.

MacNeice, Louis, *Astrology*. London: Aldus Books, 1964.

Magnusson, Magnus, *Hammer of the North*. London: Orbis Publishing, 1976.

Maple, Eric, *Magic, Medicine & Quackery*. London: Robert Hale, 1968.

Moore, Gerun, and Ruth Ericsen Setley, *Numbers Will Tell*. London: Arthur Barker, 1973.*

Morris, Ernest, collected by, *Legends o' the Bells*. London: Sampson Low, Marston, 1935.*

Neugroschel, Joachim, transl., *Great Works of Jewish Fantasy*. London: Picador, 1978.*

Newall, Venetia, *An Egg at Easter*. London: Routledge & Kegan Paul, 1971.

Oakeshott, R. Ewart, *The Archaeology of Weapons*. London: Lutterworth Press, 1960.

Oesterley, W. O. E., and G. H. Box, *The Religion and Worship of the Synagogue*. London: Sir Isaac Pitman & Sons, 1911.

Patai, Raphael, *Gates to the Old City*. Detroit: Wayne State University Press, 1981.*

Philip, J. A., *Pythagoras and Early Pythagoreanism*. Vol. 7. Toronto: University of Toronto Press, 1966.

Plato, *The Republic*. Transl. by Paul Shorey. Vol. 1, Books 1-5. London: Heinemann, 1953.

Pollard, John, *Seers, Shrines and Sirens*. London: George Allen & Unwin, 1965.

Rappoport, Angelo, S.:
The Folklore of the Jews. London: The Soncino Press, 1937.*
Myth and Legend of Ancient Israel. Vol. 3. London: The Gresham Publishing Co., 1928.*

Reinach, Salomon, *Orpheus*. Transl., rev. and partly rewritten by Florence Simmonds. New York: Liveright, 1930.

Rhys, John, *Celtic Folklore, Welsh and Manx*. Vol. 2. London: Wildwood House, 1980.*

Russell, Jeffrey B., *A History of Witchcraft*. London: Thames and Hudson, 1980.

Sébillot, Paul, *Le Folk-Lore de France*. Vol. 1. Paris: Librairie Orientale & Americaine, 1904.

Shah, Sayed Idries:
Oriental Magic. London: Rider, 1956.*
The Secret Lore of Magic. London: Frederick Muller, 1978.*

Shapiro, Max S., and Rhoda A. Hendricks, *A Dictionary of Mythologies*. London: Paladin Books, 1984.

Sikes, Wirt, *British Goblins*. London: Sampson Low, Marston, Searle & Rivington, 1880.*

Simpson, Jacqueline, *European Mythology*. Twickenham, England: The Hamlyn Publishing Group, 1987.

Simpson, Jacqueline, transl. *Legends of Icelandic Magicians*. Cambridge: D. S. Brewer Ltd. and Rowman & Littlefield for the Folklore Society, 1975.*

Southey, Robert, *Poetical Works*. London: Longmans, Green, 1880.

Storms, G., *Anglo-Saxon Magic*. The Hague: Martinus Nijhoff, 1948.*

Summers, Montague, *The Were-wolf*. London: Kegan Paul, Trench, Trubner, 1933.

Taylor, F. Sherwood, *The Alchemists*. London: Heinemann, 1951.*

Taylor, Paul B., and W. H. Auden, transls., *The Elder Edda*. London: Faber & Faber, 1969.

Thomas, Keith, *Religion and the Decline of Magic*. Harmondsworth, England: Penguin Books, 1978.

Thompson, Stith:
The Folktale. New York: The Dryden Press, 1951.
Motif-Index of Folk-Literature. 5 vols. Bloomington: Indiana University Press, 1968.*

Trigg, E. B., *Gypsy Demons and Divinities*. London: Sheldon Press, 1975.

Untermeyer, Louis, ed., *The Albatross Book of Living Verse*. London: Collins, no date.*

Vickery, Roy, ed., *Plant-Lore Studies*. London: The Foklore Society, 1984.

Vincenz, Stanislaw, *On the High Uplands*. Transl. by H. C. Stevens. London: Hutchinson, 1955.*

Wells, John Edwin, *A Manual of the Writings in Middle English, 1050-1400*. New Haven: Yale University Press, 1916.

Wheatley, Dennis, *The Devil and All His Works*. London: Hutchinson, 1971.

Wilde, Lady, *Ancient Legends, Mystic Charms, and Superstitions of Ireland*. London: Ward and Downey, 1888.*

Williams, Mary Wilhelmine, *Social Scandinavia in the Viking Age*. New York: Macmillan, 1920.

Wind, Edgar, *Pagan Mysteries in the Renaissance*. Harmondsworth, England: Penguin Books, 1967.

Zimmels, H. J., *Magicians, Theologians and Doctors*. London: Edward Goldston, 1952.

Titles marked with an asterisk were especially helpful in the preparation of this volume.

Time-Life Books Inc.
is a wholly owned subsidiary of

TIME INCORPORATED

FOUNDER: Henry R. Luce 1898-1967

Editor-in-Chief: Henry Anatole Grunwald
Chairman and Chief Executive Officer: J. Richard
Munro
President and Chief Operating Officer: N. J.
Nicholas Jr.
Chairman of the Executive Committee: Ralph
P. Davidson
Corporate Editor: Ray Cave
Executive Vice President, Books: Kelso F. Sutton
Vice President, Books: George Artandi

TIME-LIFE BOOKS INC.

EDITOR: George Constable
Executive Editor: Ellen Phillips
Director of Design: Louis Klein
Director of Editorial Resources: Phyllis K. Wise
Editorial Board: Russell B. Adams Jr., Thomas
H. Flaherty, Lee Hassig, Donia Ann Steele,
Rosalind Stubenberg, Kit van Tulleken,
Henry Woodhead
Director of Photography and Research: John
Conrad Weiser

EUROPEAN EDITOR: Kit van Tulleken
Assistant European Editor: Gillian Moore
Design Director: Ed Skyner
Chief of Research: Vanessa Kramer
Chief Sub-Editor: Ilse Gray

PRESIDENT: Christopher T. Linen
Chief Operating Officer: John M. Fahey Jr.
Senior Vice Presidents: James L. Mercer,
Leopoldo Toralballa
Vice Presidents: Stephen L. Bair, Ralph J.
Cuomo, Neal Goff, Stephen L. Goldstein,
Juanita T. James, Hallett Johnson III, Carol
Kaplan, Susan J. Maruyama, Robert H.
Smith, Paul R. Stewart, Joseph J. Ward
Director of Production Services: Robert
J. Passantino
Quality Control: James J. Cox

THE ENCHANTED WORLD

SERIES DIRECTOR: Ellen Galford
Picture Editor: Mark Karras
Designer: Lynne Brown
Series Secretary: Eugénie Romer

Editorial Staff for *The Secret Arts*
Text Editor: Tony Allan
Staff Writer: Ellen Dupont
Researcher: Lesley Colman
Assistant Designer: Julie Busby
Sub-Editor: Frances Dixon

Editorial Production
Coordinator: Maureen Kelly
Production Assistant: Deborah Fulham
Editorial Department: Theresa John,
Debra Lelliott

Correspondents: Elisabeth Kraemer-Singh
(Bonn); Maria Vincenza Aloisi (Paris);
Ann Natanson (Rome).

Chief Series Consultant

Tristram Potter Coffin, Professor of
English at the University of Pennsylvania, is a leading authority on folklore.
He is the author or editor of numerous
books and more than one hundred articles. His best-known works are *The British Traditional Ballad in North America*, *The
Old Ball Game*, *The Book of Christmas Folklore* and *The Female Hero*.

This volume is one of a series that is based
on myths, legends and folk tales.

Other Publications:

MYSTERIES OF THE UNKNOWN
TIME FRAME
FIX IT YOURSELF
FITNESS, HEALTH & NUTRITION
SUCCESSFUL PARENTING
HEALTHY HOME COOKING
UNDERSTANDING COMPUTERS
LIBRARY OF NATIONS
THE KODAK LIBRARY OF CREATIVE PHOTOGRAPHY
GREAT MEALS IN MINUTES
THE CIVIL WAR
PLANET EARTH
COLLECTOR'S LIBRARY OF THE CIVIL WAR
THE EPIC OF FLIGHT
THE GOOD COOK
WORLD WAR II
HOME REPAIR AND IMPROVEMENT
THE OLD WEST

For information on and a full description
of any of the Time-Life Books series listed
above, please write:
Reader Information
Time-Life Customer Service
P.O. Box C-32068
Richmond, Virginia 23261-2068

Library of Congress Cataloguing in
Publication Data
The Secret arts.
   (The Enchanted world)
   Bibliography: p.
   1. Tales. 2. Occult sciences.
I. Time-Life Books   II. Series
GR500.S38 1987   823'.01'0837
87-10165
ISBN 0-8094-5285-5
ISBN 0-8094-5286-3 (lib. bdg.)

Time-Life Books Inc. offers a wide range of
fine recordings, including a *Rock 'n' Roll
Era* series. For subscription information,
call 1-800-445-TIME, or write TIME-LIFE
MUSIC, Time & Life Building, Chicago,
Illinois 60611.

Tig